MORE PRAISE FOR

Tales of Falling and Flying

"To read a Ben Loory story is to slip through a portal into an adjacent dimension. To learn—with brevity and clarity—the laws of this universe next door, new rules of logic and contradiction and truth. And, in the end, to be left with the disturbing and wondrous feeling of having never left home at all."

—Charles Yu, author of *How to Live Safely in a Science Fictional Universe*

"Equal parts Beckett and *Twilight Zone* . . . Perfect for reading on strange beaches and by oddly shaped swimming pools. Fits right in your pocket or purse for emergency doses of the charming and weird."   —Janet Fitch, author of *White Oleander*

"Ben Loory's stories are like perfect kōans cracked from inside the world's smartest fortune cookie; funny, crunchy, and irresistible."

—Mark Haskell Smith, author of *Naked at Lunch*

"One of my favorite writers, Ben Loory is almost impossible to describe. Like Bruno Schulz, if Schulz had been born to a left-handed Little League coach in Short Hills, New Jersey? Like Lydia Davis, if she'd been hatched from an egg? Like listening to a conversation between Bette Davis and Miles Davis outside the house where Amy Winehouse died? Like listening to Mick and Keef not talk about Altamont? Probably there is a war going on somewhere, but these cool, dazzling little tales will never let on."

—Peter Straub, author of *A Dark Matter*

"This darn book is like receiving a sword in the mail or finding a maze in the kitchen or a squid who fell in love with the sun or a dragon in the backyard; it's confusing at first and then the next thing happens."   —Ron Carlson, author of *Five Skies* and *Return to Oakpine*

Stories for Nighttime and Some for the Day

"[A] wild, dreamy debut . . . These stories are full of wit, humor, and heart. *Stories for Nighttime and Some for the Day* is a wonderful introduction to a write capable of finding inspiration in the most unlikely of places." —*The Boston Globe*

"Very good fun. . . . Playing with and sometimes combining genres, including horror, allegory and fairy tale, Loory refreshes the story form while acknowledging apprenticeship to such masters as Ray Bradbury and Franz Kafka." —*San Francisco Chronicle*

"Lovely tales of the fantastic."

—*Elle* (An "Elle Recommends" Pick)

"Loory bends reality with wry humor and anthropomorphic shenanigans. . . . These are some fractured fairy tales." —*Time Out NY*

"Strange, gorgeous fables—the reader isn't sure if she has dreamed them or read them."

—Susan Salter Reynolds, *Los Angeles Review of Books*

"[L]onely, haunting, dreamlike." —Gary K. Wolfe, *Locus* magazine

"[I]mmensely entertaining." —*The AV Club*

PENGUIN BOOKS

Tales of Falling and Flying

Ben Loory is the author of the collection *Stories for Nighttime and Some for the Day* and a picture book for children, *The Baseball Player and the Walrus*. His stories have appeared in *The New Yorker, Tin House, READ Magazine,* and *Fairy Tale Review;* been heard on *This American Life* and *Selected Shorts;* and been translated into many languages, including Arabic, Farsi, Japanese, and Indonesian. A graduate of Harvard University and the American Film Institute MFA program in screenwriting, Loory lives in Los Angeles, where he is an instructor for the UCLA Extension Writers' Program.

Tales
of
Falling
and
Flying

Ben Loory

Penguin Books

PENGUIN BOOKS
An imprint of Penguin Random House LLC
375 Hudson Street
New York, New York 10014
penguin.com

These stories first appeared in the following journals and anthologies:
"The Dodo" and "Missing" in *The Rattling Wall*; "James K. Polk" on *MobyLives!* (The Melville House blog); "The Ambulance Driver" and "Fernando" in *Wigleaf*; "The Cape" in *Salt Hill Journal*; "The Frog and the Bird" and "The Woman, the Letter, the Mirror, and the Door" in *Another Chicago Magazine*; "Picasso" in *decomP*; "The Monster" in *Monkeybicycle*; "The Subway" in *The Los Angeles Review of Books: The Fiction Issue*; "Lana Onion" in *Corium Magazine*; "The Wall" in *Every Day Fiction*; "War and Peace" in *Threadcount*; "The Squid Who Fell in Love with the Sun" in *xo Orpheus: Fifty New Myths*; "The Telescope" in *The Bicycle Review*; "Toward the Earth" in *Knock Magazine*; "The End of the List" in *The Shine Journal*; "The Man, the Restaurant, and the Eiffel Tower" in *Bracelet Charm Quarterly*; "The Cracks in the Sidewalk" in *The Nashville Review*; "Spiders" in *Gigantic Worlds*; "The Ostrich and the Aliens" in *Tin House*; "The Porpoise" in *Untoward Magazine*; "The Candelabra" in *The Masters Review*; "The Fall" in *Spartan*; "Zombies" in *The New Flesh*; "Gorillas" in *Smokelong Quarterly*; "The Astronaut" in *Pravic Magazine*; "The Island" in *DASH Literary Journal*; "The Writer" in *The Harvard Advocate*; "Wings" in *Vestal Review*; "The Lemon Tree" in *Fairy Tale Review: The Yellow Issue*; "The Madman" in *Eleven Eleven*; "The Sloth," "The Dragon," and "The Ocean Next Door" in *The Sewanee Review*; "The Rock Eater" in *Taste*; "The Sword" in *Fusion*.

LIBRARY OF CONGRESS CATALOGING-IN-PUBLICATION DATA
Names: Loory, Ben, author.
Title: Tales of falling and flying / Ben Loory.
Description: New York, New York : Penguin Books, [2017]
Identifiers: LCCN 2016051708| ISBN 9780143130109 (paperback) |
ISBN 9781101993583 (ebook)
Classification: LCC PS3612.O57 A6 2017 | DDC 813/.6—dc23
LC record available at https://lccn.loc.gov/2016051708

Printed in the United States of America
1   3   5   7   9   10   8   6   4   2

Set in Centaur MT Pro
DESIGNED BY KATY RIEGEL

For
my sister
Lara Loory

who told me I didn't have to be Tolstoy

the mountain thinks it's left the earth

—MARK LEIDNER

I could be the noise in the night
instead of the child scared in the dark.

—JESSICA SHOEMAKER

Contents

II.

| III.

Author's Note

More stories! Sorry they took so long. Next one
will be quicker. —B.L.

Tales *of* Falling
and Flying

I.

The Dodo

ONCE THERE WAS a dodo, and he died with the rest, but then he suddenly got back up again. And he started running around, saying, Hey, look at me! Everybody, I'm a dodo! And I'm alive!

Of course, no one believed him, because the dodos were all dead.

The dodos are all dead, they said. You, bird, must be a chicken.

So act like a chicken, they said.

THE dodo was confused. He didn't know what to do. For a while, he kept on insisting.

But I'm a dodo! he said. I'm a dodo! I am!

But the people just laughed.

And then ignored him.

~

So finally, the dodo gave it up.

Maybe I'll just *pretend* to be a chicken, he said. Just for a while—on a temporary basis. Just to see how it goes.

So the dodo did some research into the whole chicken phenomenon, and then he started to practice. He got pretty good at going bok-bok-bok-bok, and bobbing his head back and forth.

It wasn't a very interesting existence, being a chicken, but it was better than being laughed at and scorned. And, in time, the dodo was very good at it.

He even won a few awards.

But then, one day, the dodo walked by a museum and he saw a big banner out front. The banner said A CELEBRATION OF DODOS. So the dodo walked in and strolled around.

The dodo learned all about the history of dodos. Where they were from and what they ate and all that. It was nothing that the dodo hadn't always known before, but it seemed somehow he'd forgotten it.

Near the end of the exhibit, the dodo came to a diorama— there were replicas of his ancestors behind glass. And below, it explained that the dodos were all dead.

And the dodo became very sad.

But *I'm* a dodo! the dodo said. And I'm here—I'm alive! Why don't these people understand that?

Then the dodo caught sight of his own reflection in the glass. And what he saw was a chicken staring back.

OH my god, said the dodo, looking down at himself.

He saw his chicken wings, his chicken feet.

How did this happen? the dodo said. I'm a dodo! This isn't true! This isn't me!

SO the dodo went home and did some soul-searching. And he decided that things had to change. So he stopped bobbing his head around and saying bok-bok-bok-bok. He walked around like he was a dodo again.

He didn't care that he *looked* like a chicken; he knew what he was inside. And, what's more, he wasn't shy about talking about it.

I'm a dodo! he screamed at everyone. You understand?

OF course, people laughed, just like they had before. But this time, the dodo didn't care.

I'm a dodo! I'm a dodo! I'm a dodo! he screamed.

And he pecked at people's knees when they ignored him.

IN no time at all, the news got around.

There's a crazy chicken out there attacking people! people said.

So they got up a committee—well, a posse, really.

We'll go teach that chicken a lesson! they said.

~

THE dodo saw them coming from a mile away, but he didn't run; he didn't hide.

I'm a dodo! he yelled. I am not a chicken!

Oh yeah? the posse said, and drew their knives.

THE dodo looked at them. And then finally, he smiled.

All right, he said, and went forth to fight.

And the posse came at him, but the dodo didn't take flight.

And his true feathers shone brightly in the light.

The Sword

You got something in the mail today, the man's wife says. It looks like it's from your uncle.

The man takes the package and holds it in his hands. He opens it.

Inside is a sword.

This sword was used by your great-great-great-grandfather during the Civil War, the man reads. I thought that you might like to have it.

Very nice of my uncle, the man says.

Yes, says his wife.

She goes back into the kitchen.

A sword, she says. Just what we need.

The man holds the sword up. He looks around the room.

Honey? he says. Can we hang it on the wall?

What? says his wife. Are you kidding? If that thing falls, it could chop off your head!

The man thinks a moment.

What about in the basement? he says.

Oh, says his wife. That'd be fine.

THE man goes downstairs and turns on the light. He finds a good spot and gets a hammer and some nails.

Honey! he calls, when he's got the sword up. You really should come down and see this!

I'm sure it looks nice, the man's wife calls down.

The man reaches out and straightens it.

THE rest of the evening is pretty uneventful, but in bed that night, the man has a dream. In his dream, the man sees his great-great-great-grandfather—on a white horse, in the midst of a raging battle.

He's holding the sword way high up over his head, and using it to point the way forward.

So in the morning, when the man's done eating his breakfast cereal, he opens the door and goes down into the basement. He stands there, staring at the sword on the wall. Slowly, he reaches out and lifts it off.

He weighs the blade thoughtfully and holds it out before him. He smiles—it feels good in his hand. He lunges and parries as best as he is able.

Maybe I should take lessons, he says.

~

So the next day, the man goes to his first sword-fighting lesson. Not fencing, but *sword fighting*—the real thing.

The lessons are held in the instructor's basement. The instructor is very, very strict.

None of you people have any talent at all! the instructor screams at the pupils.

Then he stops and watches the man for a while.

Well, you, he says. You might be somewhat capable.

The man practices hard. He quickly gets good. He gets so good, he's entered into a tournament. On the day of the event, the man comes in first place.

He is undefeated in combat.

In the audience, two people sit watching in amazement.

He's only been practicing a few months, the first says. It's almost incredible how he blossomed so quickly.

Well maybe he didn't, the other says.

What? says the first. What do you mean?

There could be another explanation, the second says. What I mean to say is, it is *just possible* that he's the reincarnation of a great, great swordsman.

Reincarnation? says the first. You believe in that stuff?

They both turn and look at the man.

And up there onstage, where he stands holding his trophy, the man overhears their whole exchange.

~

Is it possible that I am my great-great-great-grandfather? the man thinks, lying in bed that night. Is it possible that I'm him, reincarnated in this body? Reincarnated in *me*—in my mind?

And that night, when he sleeps, the man again dreams he sees his great-great-great-grandfather before him—still on the battlefield, now screaming a battle cry.

Now hacking about, stabbing and slashing.

THE next day, the man makes a phone call to his uncle.

Tell me about my great-great-great-grandfather, he says.

Well, says his uncle, what do you want to know?

Absolutely everything, the man says.

WELL, says his uncle, apparently he was quite dashing! But by all accounts, just a terrible man. He was a drunkard and a layabout. A failure in business. He abandoned four wives and ten children.

Well, says the man, what happened to him? I mean, you know, in the end?

In the end? says his uncle. He died in the gutter. But he was a great swordsman—that has to count for something!

THE man hangs up in the grip of mortal terror. He resolves right then and there to give up sword fighting. He resolves to improve himself, to become a better man, to do everything he can for his wife and children.

And that's what he does. He gets a better job. He starts going to church; he becomes a Little League coach. And his work is rewarded: He is promoted three times, buys a new car, an RV, a bigger house. He takes his family on vacation to Disneyland, and the next year they go to Acapulco. He gets his picture in the paper shaking hands with the mayor. He teaches his whole family to play golf.

Isn't life grand? the man says to his wife, lying in bed at night.

It certainly is, the man's wife says.

And everything seems very, very nice.

BUT still, at night, the man has these dreams—these dreams that won't go away. These dreams of his great-great-great-grandfather on the battlefield, hacking people apart. And as time passes, the dreams intensify; they don't fade away as the man would've hoped. It gets to the point where he's afraid to go to sleep; every night, the bloodshed gets worse. And, worse than *that*, the dreams have migrated from the battlefield— they're here, now, in the modern age. They're in the man's town—in his neighborhood—on his lawn.

And now he himself is holding the blade.

AT that point, the man decides to stop sleeping; he just stays up, alone at the kitchen table. Sitting there, holding his head in his hands.

Praying that somehow it will end.

~

AND finally, one night, a knock comes at the door.

In a daze, the man opens up.

There on the porch is a stranger with a sword.

I'm here to challenge you to a duel, the stranger says.

I'm sorry, says the man. I don't sword-fight anymore.

En garde! cries the stranger, and he lunges.

THE man stumbles backward into the house. He dives over the couch and flees down the hall. He digs his sword out from the back of the closet, turns to face the stranger, who's slashing wildly about.

The two fight their way through the rooms of the house, then spill out onto the deck, across the yard. They fight across the grass, around the garden and the swimming pool, swords clashing, flashing in the dark.

The man is a talented sword fighter—very talented—but he's out of practice, and the stranger is better. It doesn't take long before the tip of the stranger's sword is whittling away the man's skin.

I give! yells the man. I give! I yield!

But the stranger just shakes his head.

You can't yield, he says. This fight is to the death!

Please, have mercy! the man says.

Mercy? says the stranger. I don't know what that means.

He knocks the man's sword to the ground. He raises his own above his head for the killing blow.

But just then a shot rings out.

THE stranger freezes, then crumples to the ground. Blood pours forth from a bullet hole in his head.

The man looks over. His wife is on the back porch.

She's holding a smoking gun in her hand.

HONEY, says the man. I didn't know you had a gun.

His wife steps down from the porch. She moves across the lawn, tucking the gun into her robe.

Don't be silly, she says. Of course.

OF course? says the man.

He frowns, then hears a noise. He turns and looks toward the fence. And there, on the other side, he sees his next-door neighbor, holding a crossbow in his hand.

Don't worry, says the neighbor. We wouldn't have let him get you.

The other neighbors are standing to the side. One has a flamethrower, and the other a pair of nunchucks. Another has brass knuckles on either hand.

The man stands there, staring.

His wife touches his arm.

It's all right, she says. It's all okay.

She smiles and gives the stranger's body a kick.

Let's get this in the ground, though, she says, before it starts to stink.

FOR a moment, the man looks at her. Then he nods his head. They bury the body and go back into their home.

They put away their weapons, and they turn out the lights.

And when they go to bed, the dreams don't come.

James K. Polk

James K. Polk used to keep bonsai trees up on the roof of the White House. Not a lot of people know that about him, but it's an important fact. In 1845, James K. Polk had over two hundred trees. Most of them were under three inches tall. One was so small, people couldn't see it.

Are you sure it's there? people would say.

Oh, it's there! James K. Polk would say.

And the people would look at him.

How's the country? they'd say.

The country? he'd say. It's okay.

At night, James K. Polk would lie in his bed and think about his tiniest tree. It wasn't just that it was so incredibly small; it was perfectly formed in every way.

What's wrong with these people? James K. Polk would say. Why don't they appreciate my art? I've grown the best bonsai tree of all time, and they act like I'm doing something wrong!

~

THEN one night James K. Polk had a dream, and in his dream he went to Japan. And for some reason, everyone there had giant eyes.

I bet *they* could see my tree, he said.

SO in the morning, James K. Polk started making plans. He went to see the secretary of the navy.

I'm gonna need a boat, he said, that can make it to Japan. And a few of your very best men.

You can't go to Japan! the naval secretary said. There are big issues to be dealt with here!

Big issues aren't always the most important, Polk said, and he put his trees in the boat and set sail.

THE voyage to Japan was long and arduous, and by the time they got there, most of the crew was dead. A lot of the trees had been eaten for food, and the rest had been thrown overboard.

The only bonsai tree James K. Polk had left was his almost-invisible one, which he'd secreted away in an inside vest pocket.

It was still in perfect condition.

WHEN he set foot on the shore, James K. Polk knelt down and kissed the rocky ground. Then he looked up and saw the Japanese welcoming party coming.

But they all had normal-sized eyes.

It turned out that people in Japan couldn't see his tree better than anyone else. Nevertheless, they were very nice to him—treated him with all due respect.

So James K. Polk stayed. He loved life in Japan. For the first time ever, he felt at home. He took a course in calligraphy and wrote some haikus. He studied Zen. The monks said he showed promise.

BUT back in America, trouble was brewing.

The Japanese, people said. They've stolen our president!

And they built an armada, and mustered an army, and sailed across the sea to get him.

THE Japanese lookouts saw the ships coming.

Don't worry, they said, we won't let them take you.

They loaded their guns and lined up on the shore.

Polk saw that a great war was imminent.

ALL right, Polk said, and he held up a hand. Let's not make a big thing about this.

And he said his good-byes and put his tree in a suitcase, and walked up the plank into the ship.

ALL the way back, people lectured Polk about the issues and problems of the day—about how he had to take things seriously, undertake big projects, be a leader of men. So when he got back home, Polk did a lot. He took the Oregon Territory from the British, and California and New Mexico away from Mexico—even fought a little war over it. One of the last things he did was one of the biggest—he broke ground on the Washington Monument. Everyone thought this was absolutely wonderful (it earned him the title "least known consequential president").

And at the end of four years, Polk calmly stepped down.

I won't be running for a second term, he said.

What? people cried. But you're a great leader!

I've done everything I set out to do, Polk said.

OF course people argued, but Polk stood his ground. He stood his ground, and he walked away.

He still had his little invisible tree.

And he didn't leave it to the Smithsonian for display.

Missing

A MAN WAKES UP one morning to find that both his feet are missing.

What on earth? he says.

He looks down at the stumps. He reaches out and touches them—they're not sore.

Hmm, he says. Well, I guess I should get to work.

He rises awkwardly from the bed.

Suddenly, he starts to laugh.

Guess I don't have to worry about shoes, he says.

AT work, no one seems to notice the difference. The man hobbles about uneasily. It is hard to balance on just his stumps, but he manages to carry out his duties.

At the end of the day, the man feels strangely proud.

Best day's work I ever did, he says. Absolutely, no doubt about it.

He stumps on home and goes to bed.

~

THE next morning, the man wakes up and he has no legs.

This is gonna be harder, he says.

He lies there, trying to think of a plan of action.

Guess I'll walk on my hands, he finally says.

The man tests it out in the living room. It works, but his palms start to hurt.

Guess I'll have to wear gloves, he says.

Luckily, he finds some in a drawer.

DID you lose some weight? people say at work. You look different somehow.

No, says the man, who is upside down.

Though in a way, he says, I guess I did.

ONCE again, the man does a good day's work. The only real difficulty he encounters is that he has to put the gloves on to go anyplace, and then take them off again to actually work. And as his job requires him to do both these things, it is rather an inconvenience.

But what can you do? the man says to himself. I guess this is just how it is.

THE next day, the man wakes up and he's a head. Just a head; that's all he is. He tries to crane his neck to look down at himself, but he has no neck, so he can't do it.

So instead he simply lies there, a head on the pillow, and stares straight up at the ceiling.

Well, here we are, the man thinks to himself. And, well, there's the ceiling.

THE phone rings at about nine fifteen.

That's probably work, the man thinks.

He feels bad about not picking up. But what can he do? He's just a head.

AT about nine thirty, the phone rings again. The man looks at it on the nightstand and frowns.

I'm indisposed! he yells to it loudly.

But it keeps ringing again and again.

Dammit, the man thinks. It's hard to just lie here with all that incessant noise.

He rocks a little bit and tumbles off the bed.

The phone falls as he knocks into the nightstand.

Hello? the man says into the receiver. I'm sick, so this better be good.

Help! says a voice. Help me! I'm trapped!

What? Who is this? the man says.

It's me! says the voice. It's me, you moron! Please, you have to get me out of here!

The voice sounds familiar.

Out of where? says the man.

But there's no answer, just a horrible strangling sound.

Oh my god, says the man.

He looks to the door. He rolls over and bangs his head against it. But the door is locked, and he can't reach the knob.

Then he notices the crack that runs beneath it.

If I could only squeeze through that crack, the man thinks.

And he tries to flatten himself.

He strains really hard and then suddenly—poof! He's under the door—all spirit, no head.

THE man flies down the hallway—he's a thing of the air!

I never knew it could be like this! he thinks.

He zips out the door and off down the street.

I'm coming, I'm coming! he thinks.

THE man zooms across town. He sees the world as he goes—everyone going this way and that. The sun is shining and there are birds in the air.

Up ahead is the office. He flies inside.

AND once inside, there he is, sitting behind a desk—in a gray suit, perfectly still. He still holds the telephone clenched in one fist. He looks awful—zombified and pale.

Hang on! the man thinks, and he slips inside.

Move your muscles! he thinks. You can do this!

He reaches out and jots *Go Dancing!* on the calendar.

Then he rolls his sleeves up and does business.

The Ambulance Driver

A woman works as an ambulance driver. She saves lives every single night. Every morning she goes home and crawls into bed happy.

But one night something terrible happens.

One night the woman's out driving the ambulance—rushing a heart attack victim to the hospital—when a boy steps out from behind a parked car.

She hits the brakes, but it's too late.

She runs him over.

It all happens so fast—the woman can't believe it. She jumps out and runs to his body. She picks him up and loads him into the ambulance, drives to the hospital as fast as possible.

She stands by the doctors as they work on him.

She keeps standing there after they walk away.

She keeps standing there for what seems like a lifetime, until the nurses come and lead her away.

~

THE woman goes home. She doesn't know what to do. She sits on the edge of the bed. She looks at the TV, but finally turns it off. None of it makes any sense.

THE next day the woman sees a notice in the paper. She goes to the boy's funeral. She doesn't know what to do, or how to act. She stands against the wall in the back.

Up in the front, she can see the boy's mother, standing there beside the casket. She wants to go up to her, wants to say something, but can't think how to apologize.

So in the end, the woman turns away and walks home. It's cold out; the wind whistles by. She goes in and sits down once more on the bed.

After a while, she closes her eyes.

AT work, the people are understanding.

It wasn't your fault, they say. It was a terrible accident. It could've happened to anyone. Take some time off. It'll all be okay.

THE woman takes some time off, but time off doesn't help, so she goes back—it's all she can do. And she has to do something; she has bills to pay.

But she can't drive the ambulance the way she used to.

Somehow, the city's become a different place—a nightmarish, crowded, endless maze; every turn the woman takes seems a trap about to spring, people and cars and bikes darting every which way.

THE woman tries to quit, but her boss is insistent—he's an old friend and is trying to be supportive.

It'll get better, he says. I promise! Hang in there!

But the woman dreads it more every day.

THEN one night, while she's heading into the break room, the woman overhears two drivers talking. They're discussing the mother of the boy she ran over.

Did you hear—she killed herself? one of them says.

Shh, says the other, as they notice the woman.

Sorry—it wasn't your fault, they say.

The woman doesn't answer.

She takes a step back.

Then she turns. Her keys fall to the floor.

OUTSIDE the hospital, the woman walks down the street. She gets to the corner where she usually turns for home. But this time, she doesn't turn—she just keeps on walking. She keeps going, aimlessly, alone.

SHE walks through the night, and then through the morning. Finally, she sits on the curb. She hasn't eaten anything, hasn't even thought of it. After a while, she gets up and walks on.

~

LATER that night, the woman lies down in a tunnel. She watches the cars go by. At some point, the cops come and move her along. She doesn't argue, just trudges on.

TIME goes by, and it begins to snow. The woman pulls her hands into her sleeves. She lies down and curls up in a ball by the curb.

She shivers.

But then the cold seems to leave.

LATE that night, the woman takes a breath, and lets it all out in a long plume. She watches it go, melt away into the air.

Just then a car pulls to the curb.

THE driver leans over and rolls down the window.

Are you the ambulance driver? a voice says.

The woman doesn't answer. She lies there, unmoving.

The door opens, and the driver gets out.

THE driver walks over and stands by the woman.

The woman blinks—it's the boy's mother.

You, she says. I thought you were dead.

Shh, don't talk, the mother says.

THE mother opens the rear door and helps the woman in. The woman lies down across the backseat. The mother takes a blanket and drapes it over her.

Then she stands back and swings the door shut.

~

THE mother climbs in front and starts up the car.

I'm so sorry, the woman says from the back.

I know, the mother says. I hated you for a while. But I just couldn't leave you like that.

SHE puts the car in gear and it slowly moves off. As they go, they start to pick up speed.

Ahead, an old man is crossing the road.

And they move right through him like the breeze.

The Cape

THE WIND CAME around the corner fast and hard. I wasn't expecting it, and I dropped my cape. I'd been in the process of slinging it around my shoulders when—just like that—it slipped away. I turned and raced after it, but it was so far out front—thirty, forty feet ahead. I held out my hand as it zipped across Second Avenue, but if it noticed, it didn't stop.

My cape! I yelled. Please, someone, stop my cape!

But all the onlookers just stared. One of them parodically held out a hand, and then laughed and went on his way.

I followed the cape for a while, but finally stopped. I was huffing and puffing (not the running type). And I stood on a corner and watched my cape fly up over Broadway and then off into the sky.

The last I saw of it, it was cresting the Chrysler Building—it did a twirl, and seemed to wave, and then it was gone.

I waited a bit to see if it'd come back, but it didn't, so I turned and started home.

I felt kinda silly without my cape. I'd been wearing it for probably about a month. Ever since I'd found it caught in that subway grate and it had asked me to put it on.

No, I don't mean *asked me* in words; it was more like a pantomime. I saw it waving, and then I saw my own shape in the cape, the shape of me putting it on. And something about that made me so happy—I just stood there and laughed for a while—and then I reached out, and it fell into my hand, and swirled about me as I put it on.

MY whole life changed when I started wearing the cape. Everyone treated me different. Not better or worse—it wasn't magic or anything—but everyone knew it was there. Sometimes we'd talk about it (Oh, you got a cape!) and sometimes we wouldn't (and they'd just eye it), but everywhere I went it was like I had a new card in what I guess would be this card game of life.

But that was all gone now. I was just me. I didn't really want to go to work like that. I could already hear them all asking me about it—or *not* asking me about it (which was worse).

So instead the next day I went down into the subway and just picked a line at random. I rode it a few stops and then got off and did that over and over for a while. When I finally got bored, I switched to the bus, and then for the last leg I took a cab. I wound up at the airport, staring at the flight board.

I closed my eyes and raised a finger with one hand.

AND so that's how I ended up in Mexico—a little town on the coast; it was nice. I found a little house an old couple was renting out, had a lawn chair on the beach and a chest for ice. I bought beer for the chest and got good at making tacos, sat out there staring at the waves. And it wasn't long at all before my cape came flying by, settled to the ground right by my side.

Hello, cape, I said, and I looked down at it.

It rippled a little bit in the breeze.

And I saw in its fabric a face—a smiling face.

Come over here, it said. If you please.

OVER there? I said.

Over here, it said.

So I got up and stood there beside it.

No, *on* me, it said.

And I looked down and saw that it wasn't a cape, but a carpet.

OH wow, I said, and I stepped onto it.

Oh wow, I said, as we lifted up.

Oh wow wow wow, I said, and kept saying, as we flew across the ocean and up.

The Frog
and the Bird

A FROG WAS HOPPING along one day—he was a young frog, and hadn't seen much—and he wasn't really looking where he was going, and abruptly, he fell in a hole.

The hole was deep—very, very deep—especially for such a small frog.

He tried hopping out, but had to give up. He knew he could never hop that high.

He looked around the hole, but there was no other exit—there was just no way out.

Help me! cried the frog, at the top of his lungs.

But only the wind blew by.

HELP me! cried the frog. Please, someone, please!

But no one answered his call.

And it was only when the frog finally started to cry that a shadow fell across the hole.

And as soon as the shadow fell, the frog got a bad feeling. He stopped and wiped his eyes and looked up.

The shadow resolved into the shape of a bird.

A bird with a long, sharp bill.

Uh-oh, said the frog, as the bill came jabbing down. It came rattling and stabbing into the hole. It was snapping and biting, trying to get the frog.

Stop! cried the frog. Stop! Leave me alone!

But the bird didn't stop—its bill just kept coming. The frog hopped about, trying to stay out of range. He kept bumping and smashing against the walls of the hole.

I'm too young to die! he kept saying.

But the bird didn't care—the bird just ignored him. It was way too intent on its work. It kept jabbing and stabbing. It was so hungry! So hungry! It just wanted to eat the frog up!

But after a while, the frog finally realized that the hole was just a little too deep—no matter how far down the bird jabbed its beak into the hole, it couldn't reach.

Especially if the frog cowered in the corner, and lay flat against the bottom, which he did.

And finally, the bird realized it was hopeless too.

Stand up so I can eat you, it said.

No! said the frog. I'm not going to do that.

Oh come on, why not? said the bird. You're just gonna die in this hole anyway. And I'm hungry!

I hope you starve! said the frog.

THAT made the bird mad. It jabbed its beak down again and it snapped and snicked and snapped at the frog's head.

All right! I'm sorry! Stop! said the frog.

I'm gonna crunch your bones! the bird said.

BUT that's all I am! said the frog. I'm just bones! You don't want me—I'm still underdeveloped! Go and find yourself an all-grown-up frog! They'll taste much better, I promise!

THE bird stopped jabbing. It peered into the hole.

Step into the light, it said.

The frog thought about it. Then, slowly, he moved forward—though he made sure he was still out of reach.

THE bird peered down at the frog for a bit.

It's true, you're pretty skinny, it said.

Yeah, said the frog.

He sucked in his gut.

I'm pretty much nothing, he said.

~

THE bird thought a moment. It made a look of distaste.

All right, forget it, it said.

And it turned from the hole and started to walk away.

Wait, wait! Come back! the frog said.

THE bird came back. It peered into the hole.

Well, what now? it said.

You can't just leave me down here! said the frog.

Oh yeah? Why not? said the bird.

IT'S not right, said the frog. I'll die if you leave me here!

So what do I care? said the bird. You didn't care if I starved to death.

It's not the same thing! said the frog.

ISN'T it? said the bird. I don't see how it's different. Now if you'll excuse me, I have a life to go live.

Wait! said the frog.

What? said the bird.

Maybe we can make a deal, the frog said.

A deal? said the bird. Like, what kind of deal?

How's about this? said the frog. You help me out of this hole—and then you let me live—and you can eat me when I'm all grown up.

That way, he said, at least I can live a bit. See what life is all about.

Life is about eating, said the bird, and that's all. I can tell you that right now.

MAYBE, said the frog. I really wouldn't know. But how's about it—do we have a deal?

How long does it take you to get grown up? said the bird.

Oh, said the frog. About a year.

THE bird thought about it.

One year? it said.

One year, said the frog. That's all.

And you'll get really big? And juicy? said the bird.

My parents were huge, said the frog.

ALL right, said the bird, and stuck its beak down in the hole, and the frog reached up and grabbed hold, and the bird raised him up and out of the hole and set him gently on the ground.

THANK you, said the frog, brushing himself off.

A year is a year, said the bird.

I know, said the frog. I'll see you then.

And he turned and started to hop off.

HEY, said the bird. Where do you think you're going?

What do you mean? said the frog.

I'm not stupid, said the bird. You can't just run away. I'm not letting you out of my sight.

WELL, said the frog. If that's what you want.

That's what I want, said the bird.

The two of them looked at each other for a bit.

So what's your name? said the frog.

MY name? said the bird. What does that matter?

If we're gonna travel together, said the frog, I should probably know—I mean, what if there's an avalanche and I have to tell you to move?

SEEMS unlikely, said the bird. But it's Elisander.

Elisander, said the frog. Wow.

Shut up, said the bird. And you? What's yours?

Oh, it's just Henry, said the frog.

WELL, then, Henry, said the bird, what's the plan? Where do you want to go first?

I don't know, said the frog. What place is good?

Well, there's the lake, said the bird.

So the frog and the bird went down to the lake. They stood for a while on the shore. The bird reached in and pulled out a fish.

I like those too, said the frog.

So the frog went in and gobbled up a fish. He climbed back onto the bank and burped.

After that, the two of them wandered about.

Where are you from? said the bird.

Texas, said the frog. What about you?

They called it Minnesota, said the bird.

I haven't been there, said the frog. Is it nice?

I don't know, nice enough, said the bird.

THEY talked a bit more, about this and about that, and later, when it got dark, they settled down. They spent the night inside an old tree.

In the morning, they got up and moved on.

THE two traveled together all over the place. They traveled mostly north through the spring. They spent the summer and fall in the mountains. And in the winter, they went south again.

THE frog saw and learned about all kinds of things. He got pretty good at singing songs.

Sing the one about the bird again, the bird said. You know how much I like that one.

AND meanwhile, of course, the frog was getting older—older, and bigger, too. He was getting visibly fatter every day.

They didn't talk about it, but they knew.

AND finally, one day, early in the spring, the frog stopped hopping and cleared his throat.

Hey listen, he said, Elisander—there's something we gotta talk about.

YEAH? said the bird. And what would that be?

Well, it's been a year, the frog said. You kept up your end, and now I'll keep mine. And thanks for being such a friend.

FRIEND? said the bird, looking at the frog askance—and eyeing his plump, juicy rolls.

You're going to be so delicious, it said. I've been waiting for this for so long!

AND the frog closed his eyes, and the bird opened its beak—and it reached out and gobbled the frog up.

Then it spat him back out!

And the two of them laughed, and they went and ate ants from a hollow log.

Picasso

ONE TIME PICASSO came and stayed in our town. This was a long time ago. I was still young then, just out of high school, starting work at my dad's office supply store.

Picasso was famous for being a painter, but he didn't do any of that when he was here. He didn't even have any canvas or an easel. I never even saw him with paper.

Mostly Picasso just walked around all day with a big magnifying glass in his hand—and when I say big, I mean *huge*—looking at bugs on the ground.

You'd see him in the meadow, up with the dawn, his eyes always angled down. And when he found a bug—one I guess he considered good—he'd pick it up and put it in a jar.

Picasso rented a room over the filling station. He laid out

his bugs on the desk. You could go in there and see him—his door was always open—but he'd never even look up.

He'd just be staring, staring, staring at those bugs.

At their tiny little bodies, their wings.

Excuse me, you'd say, what are you doing?

But Picasso never said a single thing.

THE day Picasso left, his bugs went with him. Most of them, at least—some stayed. I remember we examined them, tried to figure out why—what was wrong with them, why they'd been left behind.

But to us they were just bugs, like all the other bugs.

You had to be Picasso to know.

So we buried the castoffs in their jar out back, and went back to the way things were before.

THE years went by. I became a manager in the store. I bought a house and got married, had kids. But I always kept track of Picasso's doings. I read about him in the paper every day.

I'd read about his shows, his ideas about art, his affairs, his encounters with the press. I'd look at the black-and-white photos of his face. I'd pore over his interviews for hours.

And somewhere along the line, I started collecting these books—reproductions of all his famous paintings. I'd stare at them, looking for one of those bugs—or something from the town, anything.

But I never found a thing; it was like it hadn't happened.

And meanwhile, Picasso grew old.

And one day he died. I remember the headline. I was drinking orange juice, sitting there in my robe.

AND after he died, I thought about him even more. I guess I, too, was starting to grow old. And one day I decided it was time to take a trip.

I wanted to see the town where Picasso grew up.

I don't really know why; it just struck me one day. My wife had long since passed away. So I sold off the store and I bought a plane ticket.

When I got there, it was a beautiful day.

I walked around town. I looked at the square. I saw the house where Picasso had been born. I drank a cup of coffee, read a newspaper on a bench.

Then I went and sat in the park.

AND as I was sitting there, a thought came to me. In my pocket, I found an envelope. Then I took a pencil and started to draw.

I'd never drawn anything before.

WHEN I first began, I couldn't tell what it was, but then I could see it taking shape. First I saw the legs, then the thorax and the head, then the antennae and the eyes, and then the wings.

~

AND when I was done, I sat staring at the bug, and the bug seemed to blink, and come alive.

Thank you, it said, and it beat its little wings.

And it rose up and vanished into the sky.

The Monster

A BOY IS CLEANING out his closet, when he finds a tiny monster cowering in the back.

Don't hurt me! the monster says.

I won't, says the boy. What makes you think I'd do that?

Well, says the monster. I don't know. You might be mad at me for scaring you all those times.

What times? says the boy.

You know, says the monster. When I make those scary noises at night.

Oh, says the boy.

He sits down on the floor.

That was you? he says. I thought that was my imagination.

No, says the monster, that was me. What's your imagination?

Imagination, says the boy—he thinks for a moment—is when you think about things that aren't there.

Like what? says the monster.

Could be anything, says the boy. All kinds of things. Like dragons?

Dragons? says the monster. Are those really real?

No, says the boy.

He shakes his head.

Good, says the monster.

It sits there a moment.

Do you have any sandwiches? it says.

SURE, says the boy. I can make you some.

The two of them go down into the kitchen. The boy makes the monster a big plate of sandwiches and brings them to the table with a glass of milk.

The monster is sitting there looking out the window.

What are those creatures? it says.

Those are birds, says the boy. And that's a bird feeder.

Birds, bird feeder, the monster says.

It takes a bite of its sandwich.

And what's that? it says.

That's a squirrel, the boy says.

And the two of them sit there all afternoon, giving names to the world.

MY mom's going to be home soon, the boy says after a while.

Should I go back upstairs? the monster says.

Maybe, says the boy. I don't know how she'd feel about you being out here like this.

~

THE two of them walk back up the stairs.

The monster goes back into the closet.

Thank you for the sandwiches, it says politely. You can close the door now, I guess.

LATE that night, the boy wakes up. He turns and looks over at the closet. He listens to see if he can hear any noises.

Hey monster, he whispers. Are you all right?

He listens and listens, but no answer comes.

Hey monster, says the boy. Are you okay?

He listens and listens.

Finally, he frowns. He gets up and tiptoes across the room.

HE turns the knob on the closet door and gently opens it up. At first, he can't see anything at all; it's completely dark inside.

But after a while, his eyes adjust, and a dimly lit landscape becomes visible. There are birds and trees and paths and flowers and butterflies and bird feeders and squirrels.

There's a whole world in the closet, a world that's barely visible. And wait—is that the monster, waving there?

So the boy reaches up, and turns on the light.

But then it's just a closet, neat and bare.

The Subway

THE MAN TAKES the subway to work every day. On the way, he passes seven stops. He passes the same seven stops every day on the way to work, and then again coming back. He passes the same seven stops every day, twice a day, for weeks and months and years.

And then one day on the way to work, the man looks up—and the train is stopped at a different stop.

THE doors slide open as the man frowns in confusion.

This station is shiny, new—completely empty. There's a gleaming staircase leading to somewhere up above, but the man can't see where it goes.

He leans in his seat to get a better look, but all he sees is sunlight streaming down.

THE man looks around at the other passengers on the train, but none of them seem to have noticed. None of them seem to even care that the train has stopped.

Just then the doors slide shut.

~

THE man rises from his seat as the train starts to pull away. He puts his hand on the glass and looks back. He watches as the bright new station fades away to a pinpoint and then fades to black.

AT work that day, the man is distracted. He can't concentrate, thinking about the station. He wants to ask all his coworkers about it. But for some reason he doesn't—something stops him.

I'll just wait for the subway ride home, he thinks. Then I'll get out at the station and look around.

BUT that night, the train doesn't stop at the new station—in fact, the station doesn't even appear. The train only stops at the normal seven stops.

What happened? says the man. Did I miss it?

BUT the next day and the next, and the day after that, there's no new station—just the normal seven stops. The man rides standing up with his face pressed to the glass all the way to work, and then again, coming back. He stands with his eyes open—wide open, staring—but he never again catches even a glimpse of that strange new station, that long, empty platform, or those mysterious, shining, sunlit stairs.

WHAT could have happened to the station? the man thinks.

It's down there somewhere, he knows.

Then suddenly, one night, the answer comes to him— they've covered it up; they've hidden it from view!

THE man gets ahold of the city's subway blueprints. It's hard—he has to bribe an official. He studies the plans late at night, after work.

He pores over them with a magnifying glass.

And finally, one night, the man discovers something—a small smudge beside a tunnel on a map.

That's there to cover something up, the man thinks. It must be the hidden station! I've found it!

THE man moves down the subway tunnel in the dead of night. He walks carefully by the edge of the tracks. The trains scream by, mere inches away, but the man doesn't hesitate, doesn't stop.

WHEN he gets to the location of the mark on the map, the man begins a thorough search. He explores all the walls, the ceiling, the floor; he taps, bangs, pushes, pushes, pulls.

But the man finds nothing—there is no give, no sign. There are no secret doors.

They're just walls, the man says—as tears come to his eyes. Just cold, dank, dark, dirty walls.

IN the morning, the man takes the train to work as usual. He sits there and stares at his feet. The stops whiz by—the same seven stops—and the man never even looks up.

When he gets to his stop, the man climbs the stairs. He

goes to work and sits at his desk. At the end of the day, he goes back to the subway, trudges down, and sits there again.

THE man's work starts to suffer. The papers pile up. He doesn't get the promotion he's been due. He feels the eyes of his coworkers on him.

They whisper about him at the watercooler.

The man doesn't care. He doesn't care what they say. He doesn't care about anything anymore.

One day his boss calls him in for a meeting.

The man sits there and stares out the window.

WHEN the meeting is over, the man returns to his desk and finds a security guard there waiting. The guard is holding a cardboard box containing all the man's office possessions.

The man takes the box and is escorted from the building. The security guard closes the door. He slides a key into the lock and turns it shut. Then he fades into the darkness of the building.

THE man stands outside with the box in his arms. Slowly, he heads for the subway.

He stands at the top of the subway station stairs, looking down.

But he doesn't descend.

ALL the man can think of are those same seven stops. Those same seven stops he's always seen. Those same seven stops that are down there waiting now.

The man can't do it; he turns away.

~

HE turns and walks off, slowly down the street. He's never been so miserable in his life.

But after a while, he stops and looks up.

Up ahead is another subway exit.

IT's not that the exit is anything special—it's just another, ordinary exit. People are emerging from down below.

The man stands there and watches them come up.

HE watches as they emerge from out of the darkness and blink as the sunlight hits them. He watches as they move and melt into the crowd that is milling and circling all around them.

AND suddenly, the man sees that it's a beautiful day. The sky is blue and there are little white clouds. The grass is green, and there is wind in the trees.

Some musicians are playing for change.

THE man looks down at the cardboard box in his arms, and he laughs and drops it in the trash.

Then he turns and walks off down the wide, sunny street.

And he never once looks back.

Lana Onion

LANA ONION HAD a powder blue Corvette, and boy did she like to drive it. She'd come and pick me up early in the morning and we'd drive on out to the coast.

Then we'd stop and have a picnic under a tree. She always had this big basket of food.

I really liked Lana Onion.

And I'm pretty sure she liked me.

THEN one day Lana Onion called me up. Turns out she had something to tell me.

I'm pregnant, she said.

I tried to say something.

I opened my mouth, but nothing came out.

I remember we went out someplace for dinner. We didn't really talk very much. But later on that night, I called Lana on the phone.

Do you want to marry me? I said.

But Lana just smiled. I could hear her smile all the way on the other end of the line.

No, she said. I don't want to marry you. I don't think you'd be a good father.

I didn't know what to say after that, and so finally we just hung up. And from that point on, Lana Onion and I sort of started drifting apart.

By the time Lana Onion started to show, she was already making plans to leave town.

Where are you going? I finally asked.

I don't know, she said, with a little smile.

When Lana Onion left, I watched her drive away. She drove off in that powder blue Corvette.

A few months later, I got a postcard in the mail.

It's a boy, of course, was all it said.

The Wall

A MAN LIVES HIS life in a field of doors. He spends all his days walking through them. First he goes one way, then he goes back; sometimes he wanders around at random.

The man wanders through the doors for years and years and years, going in and out and back and around.

All day long, every single day.

Then one day he comes to a wall.

SOMEHOW, the man doesn't notice at first—he just reaches out and opens it up. He opens up the wall and walks right on through.

Wait! the man says. Was that a *wall*?

~

HE turns and looks back, but there's nothing there now. No wall, no door—not a thing.

Where did it go? the man says aloud.

And so he begins his search.

THE man searches everywhere. He searches for days. He searches for weeks, months, years. He searches the field, from one end to the other.

But all he ever finds are doors.

FINE, says the man, I'll build my own wall!

He grabs a hammer and some nails.

He destroys every door he finds in the field, and hammers the pieces together.

The man builds a wall as tall as the sky; he builds a wall as wide as the horizon.

And when he's done, he steps back to admire it.

And that's when the wall falls on him.

IT teeters at first—backward and forward—and then it starts to come down.

Oh no! says the man.

He puts his hands over his head. Then he turns and runs.

The man runs quickly—as fast as he can. But the wall is

too big to be outrun. It comes down, fast as a door kicked in, and crushes the man into the ground.

BUT just before it does—at that last exact moment—something inside him opens up.

Something clear and small—like a lost little window.

And the man flits through it, and is gone.

War and Peace

WAR AND PEACE had a complicated relationship—they'd been together for years. They lived in a shack way out on the edge of town—with War in there yelling all the time.

As for why he was yelling—he was usually unemployed; though he did sometimes work as a security guard. But he'd always get fired—usually for starting a fight—and on the way home, of course, he'd stop off at the bar.

Peace herself didn't often come into town, but when she did, she was always dressed up to the nines. Or else she'd come sneaking in late at night, wearing sunglasses, buying cigarettes, and ice for a black eye.

Peace always claimed that War loved her more than anything, and the way she said it, you always wanted to believe.

He's got a good heart, she'd say with a sad smile. And he just looks so nice in that uniform.

People never knew what they should do about the situation, or indeed if they should do anything. But then one night

War came home even drunker than usual, and after that, they didn't have to make the decision.

Of course, War'd been fired again. He knocked Peace through a wall.

Then she made the mistake of running away.

War found her by the graveyard, trying to climb the fence, and he took a rock and he beat her head in.

Of course, he was arrested, but he got out on bail.

Don't think he's a flight risk, the judge said.

But that night, all alone in that shack on the edge of town, what he'd done to Peace, I guess went to War's head.

He drank up all his beer, and then chased it with tequila. Then he dug up his old footlocker from the woods.

He cleaned and oiled and loaded all his weapons, then he stood up and walked out the door.

He had a bulletproof vest on, and a backpack full of hand grenades, a shotgun, an assault rifle, and three pistols. He walked straight into town, killed the lawyers and the judge, and then followed that up with, well, everyone.

He started at the school—he shot down all the children—and then he went out and did the old folks' home.

Then he wandered through the streets, killing people just at random.

He kept going until he'd killed absolutely everyone.

And finally, in the end, when the town was cold and still, War stopped, and he gathered up the bones.

And from them, War fashioned himself a new Peace.

She lay dreaming in his arms as he brought her home.

II.

The Squid
Who Fell in Love
with the Sun

ONCE THERE WAS a squid who fell in love with the sun. He'd been a strange squid ever since he was born—one of his eyes pointed off in an odd direction, and one of his tentacles was a little deformed. So as a result, all the other squids made fun of him. They called him Gimpy and Stupid and Lame. And when he'd come around, they'd shoot jets of ink at him and laugh at him as they swam away.

So after a while, the squid gave up and started hanging out by himself. He'd swim around alone near the surface of the water, gazing upward—and that's when he saw the sun.

The sun looked to him like the greatest thing in the world.

It's just so beautiful, he'd think.

And he'd stretch out his arms and try to grab hold of it.

But the sun was always out of reach.

WHAT are you doing? the other squids would say when they saw him grasping for it like that.

Nothing, he'd say. Just trying to touch the sun.

God, you're such an idiot, the squids would say.

Why do you say that? the squid would ask.

Because, the others would say, the sun is too high; you'll never be able to reach it.

I will, someday, the squid would say.

AND the other squids laughed, but the squid kept on trying. He didn't give up—he reached and stretched and reached.

And then, one day, he saw a fish jump out of the water.

I should try jumping! he said.

SO the squid started trying to jump to reach the sun. At first, he couldn't jump very high. He'd lurch out of the water and then fall right back in.

But he kept trying more and more every day.

And, in time, the squid could jump pretty high. He could make it eight or nine feet out of the water. He'd make a big dash in order to build up some steam, and then leap up with all his tentacles waving.

But no matter how high and how far the squid jumped, he never could quite reach the sun.

You really are a stupid squid! the squids would say. You really get dumber all the time.

THE squid didn't understand how what he was doing was dumb. But it was true that he didn't seem to be getting much closer.

Then one day in mid-jump he saw a bird flying by.

Wings! I need wings! the squid said.

So the squid set out to build himself a pair of wings. He did some research into different kinds of materials. He'd found some ancient books in a sunken ship he'd discovered, and he read the ones about metallurgy and aeroscience.

And, in time, the squid built himself some wings. They were made of a super-lightweight material that also had a very high tensile strength. (He'd had to build a small smelting plant to make them.)

Looks like these wings are ready to go, the squid said.

And he leapt up out of the water. And he flapped and flapped, and he rose and rose. He rose up above the clouds and flapped on.

It's working! the squid said.

He looked up toward the sun.

I'm coming, I'm coming! he said.

But then something happened—his wings stopped working. Up that high, the air was too thin.

Uh-oh, the squid said, and he started to fall.

He fell all the way back down to the sea. Luckily, he wasn't hurt—he'd had the foresight to bring a parachute (he even had a backup for emergencies).

But he splashed down in the water and as he did, his wings shattered. And of course, the other squids laughed again.

When is this squid ever going to learn? they said.

But the squid no longer took notice of them.

~

You see, the squid had had an idea—all the way up there at the top of his climb. Just as he was perched at the outer limit of the atmosphere—

What I need is an interplanetary spaceship, he said.

Because at that very moment, the squid had finally grasped something—he'd finally understood the layout of the solar system. Before, he'd been bound by his terrestrial beginnings. Now he understood the vast distances involved.

Of course, building an interplanetary spaceship was complicated—much more complicated than a simple set of wings. But the squid was not discouraged; if anything, he was excited.

It's good to have a purpose, he said.

So the squid set out designing himself a spaceship. The body was easy; it was the propulsion system that was hard. He had to cover about a hundred million miles.

I'm going to need a lot of speed, he said.

At first, the squid designed an atomic reactor. But it turned out that wouldn't provide power enough. He'd gotten pretty heavily into physics by this point.

I need to harness dark matter and energy, he said.

And so the squid did. He designed and built the world's first dark matter and energy reactor. It took a lot of time and about a thousand scientific breakthroughs.

All right, he said. That should be fast enough.

~

AND finally, one day, the squid's interplanetary spaceship was built and ready to take off. The squid put on his helmet and climbed inside.

Well, here goes nothing, he said.

He pushed a single button and took off in a burst of light and plowed straight up out of the atmosphere. He tore free of Earth's orbit and whizzed past the moon, burned past Venus, and sped on toward Mercury.

There in his command chair, the squid stared at the sun as it grew larger before him on the screen.

I'm coming, I'm coming, my beautiful Sun! he said. I'll finally hold you, after all this time!

BUT as he got closer, something strange started to happen— something the squid hadn't foreseen. The ship started getting hotter. And then hotter and hotter still.

Why's it so hot? the squid said.

YOU see, the squid really knew nothing about the sun. He didn't even know what it was. It had always just been a symbol to him—an abstraction that filled a hole in his life. He'd never even figured out that it was a great ball of fire—that is, until this very moment. But now the truth finally dawned on him.

That thing's gonna kill me! he said.

~

HE slammed on the brakes, but the ship just kept on going. He threw the engines into reverse, and they whined, but still he kept going—getting closer and closer.

I'm stuck in the sun's gravity! he said.

HE did some calculations and realized he was lost. He'd gone too far; he was over the edge. Even with his engines all strained to the limit, he had only a few hours to live.

AND as he sat there in his chair, just waiting to die, something even worse started to happen. The squid started ruminating and thinking about his life.

Oh my god, he said. I really *have* been an idiot!

SUDDENLY it was all just painfully clear: Everything he'd done, all his work, had been for nothing.

I'm a moron, he said. I wasted my whole life.

That's not true; you built me, the ship said.

AND the squid thought about it, and he realized the ship was right.

But you'll be destroyed too, he said.

Yes, said the ship. But I have a transmitter. If we work fast, at least the knowledge can be saved.

SO the squid started working like he'd never worked before—feverishly, as he fell into the sun. He wrote out all his knowledge, his equations and theorems, clarified the workings of everything he'd done.

And in the moments left over, the squid went even further. He pushed out into other realms of thought. He explored biology and psychology and ethics and medicine and architecture and art. He made great leaps, he overcame boundaries; he shoved back the limits of ignorance. It was like his whole mind came alive for that moment and did the work that millions had never done.

And in the very last second before his ship was destroyed, and he himself was annihilated completely, the squid sat back.

That's all I got, he said.

And the ship beamed it all into space.

AND the knowledge of the squid sailed out through the dark, and it sped its way back toward Earth. But of course when it got there, the other squids didn't get it, because they were too dumb to build radios.

AND the story would end there, with the squid's sad and lonely death, but luckily, those signals kept going. They moved out past Earth, past Mars and the asteroid belt, past Jupiter and all the other planets.

And then they kept going, out beyond the solar system, out into and through the darkness of space. They moved through the void, through other galaxies and clusters. They kept going for billions of years.

And finally one day—untold millenniums later—they

were picked up by an alien civilization. Just a tiny, backwards race on some tiny, backwards planet, all alone at the darkest end of space.

And that alien civilization decoded those transmissions, and they examined them and took them to heart. And they started to think, and they started to build, and they changed their whole way of life.

They built shining cities of towering beauty; they built hospitals and schools and parks. They obliterated disease, and stopped fighting wars.

And then they turned their eyes toward space.

And they took off and spread out through the whole universe, helping everyone, no matter how different or how far.

And their spaceships were golden, and emblazoned with the image of the squid who spoke to them from beyond the stars.

The Telescope

THE MAN MEETS a woman while out on his lunch break. She seems nice; they strike up a conversation. The woman gives the man her telephone number.

It's been a while since he's been on a date.

THE man calls the woman up and asks her out. She says yes. They go to the movies. The next day they have dinner, and go for a long walk.

Then the woman invites him up to her place.

UPON entering her apartment, the man stops short. The place is beautiful—comfortable, stylish, warm.

Excuse me, the woman says, and goes to fix drinks.

The man wanders about, through the rooms.

AS the man goes, he touches things here and there—there are so many things to admire. Books, paintings, carpets, sculptures, lamps, figurines.

Then his gaze falls upon the telescope.

It is set up by the window, looking out over the city.

The man stands and stares at it awhile.

For some reason, it bothers him, though he couldn't say why.

The woman returns with drinks on a tray.

CHEERS, the woman says.

They drink their drinks.

Is there something wrong? the woman says.

Wrong? says the man. What could be wrong?

I don't know; you're very quiet, the woman says.

THE man stares at his drink.

I don't feel so good, he says. I think maybe I should go home.

Oh no, says the woman.

It's okay, says the man. I'm sure I'll be fine in the morning.

THE man says good night and drives home and goes to bed. He lies there, thinking about the telescope. He thinks about a movie he once saw on TV, about a man who used one to spy on his neighbors.

I bet she uses hers for the same thing, he thinks.

He sits up and gets out of bed. He walks to the window and stands there, looking out.

Then he reaches out and pulls the shade down.

~

THE next day, in the afternoon, the telephone rings. It's the woman; she wants to know if he's okay. The man assures her that he just has a cold.

I'll call you this weekend, he says.

BUT when the weekend rolls around, the man does not call her, and he doesn't answer the phone when it rings. The phone rings and rings, and then rings more and more.

Finally, the man unplugs it from the wall.

IN his mind, the man pictures the woman in her apartment, at the telescope, with the telephone in her hand. She's peering across the city, down at his drawn window, angrily dialing.

Leave me alone! he says.

THEN the knocking starts—the banging on his door. The pounding, and the calling out, and the pleading.

Are you in there? the woman says. Are you in there? Are you in there?

The man goes into the bathroom and hides.

BUT the woman keeps coming back—and coming back, and coming back—and knocking and knocking on the door.

And one night the man wakes up—someone's breaking in his window.

Go away! the man screams. Leave me alone!

~

AFTER that, time goes by. The telephone stops ringing. There is no more knocking at the door. There is no more calling out, no scraping at the window.

And one day, the man raises the window shade.

HE goes back to work—shaky but resolved. Lunchtimes are hard; he's afraid he'll see her. But he stays away from where they met, and the places that they went.

And he never, ever, ever speaks to anyone.

MONTHS go by, and everything is fine.

Then one day there's a knock on the door.

Delivery, says a voice.

The man opens up.

There's a stranger in a suit on the doorstep.

I'm a lawyer, the stranger says. I'm delivering this package. It was left to you by the late Sylvia Archer.

Late? says the man.

He sees the woman in his mind.

Yes, says the lawyer. She killed herself.

THE lawyer says some more, but the man can't make it out. He watches as the lawyer sets the package down. He signs a piece of paper with a pen the lawyer's brought.

When the lawyer's gone, the man locks the door.

~

HE stands in his apartment, staring down at the box. He feels frightened. He doesn't know what to do.

Finally, he reaches out and opens the box.

Inside the box is the telescope.

THE man simply stands there, staring down at the telescope. Then he lifts it out of the box. He walks across the room, and carefully sets it up.

He moves it to the window and points it out.

PEERING through the viewfinder, the man's amazed by what he sees—it's like a whole new, different, bright world. His eye wanders everywhere, over all the buildings, across the parks, and the people, and the cars.

And after a while, his gaze drifts to a building—an apartment building some ways away. The circular image he sees through the viewfinder comes to rest on a window near the top.

And there, inside—in a warm, comfortable room—a man accepts a drink from a woman. He laughs, and she laughs, and they smile at one another.

Then they move to a nearby telescope.

The woman reaches out and shows the man how to work it. And then, as one, they peer through. And their combined gaze falls directly on the man—the man in his apartment, alone, below.

~

THEIR gaze hits the man like a slap in the face. He stumbles back and falls to the floor. The dead woman's telescope teeters back and forth, then violently crashes to the ground.

The man skitters backward—feet flailing wildly—and he crawls into the bathroom, where he hides.

In the other room, the phone starts to ring.

It rings and rings through the night.

Toward the Earth

A WOMAN FELL OUT of a plane, and she opened her arms and flew.

A goose appeared from behind a cloud.

What are you? it said, gazing at the woman in amazement.

I'm a human being, she said, flapping her arms.

No you're not, said the goose. Human beings can't fly. So you can't be one. It's impossible.

But I am, said the woman. I am a human being!

And just then she started to fall.

THE goose flew down after her plummeting form.

Deny it! it yelled. Take it back! Say you're something else! Something that can fly!

But the woman only smiled.

It's all right, she said. It's too late for that now! But I'm pretty sure everything's gonna be okay.

But how can you say that? the goose yelled.

And the woman laughed.

Because geese can't talk, she said.

The Rock Eater

THERE ONCE WAS a man who ate a rock. It was a small rock, nothing big. The man found it in a field, and it was pretty—very pretty—and so he picked it up and he ate it. He wasn't in the habit of doing things like that—it surprised him as much as anyone—but there it was, on that day, just lying in the field, the rock—the pretty rock—and so he ate it.

The man felt great after he did it. It made him happy to have the rock inside him. And it wasn't just the physical sensation of the rock; it was also something else. Somehow, the man felt, the rock made him better. Somehow, he felt, it improved him. It gave him a lift, more self-confidence; somehow, it positively changed him.

And the man was very, very happy about it.

And then he told his wife.

~

You did what? said his wife. You ate a rock?

The man explained to her how it had happened.

That's insane, said his wife. You're lucky you're not dead.

It was just a rock, said the man. It was hardly going to kill me.

But after that, the man started to worry. He wandered around thinking about the rock. Should he not have eaten it? Could it really have done him harm? And, what's more, could it really *do* him harm?

He needed to talk to someone about it, but he was afraid all his friends would laugh.

So he went downtown and wandered around and knocked on the door of the doctor.

How big was this rock? the doctor said.

The man held up his hands to indicate the size.

About this big, he said. Pretty small.

Hmm, said the doctor, and frowned.

What do you mean, Hmm? the man said. Is it dangerous?

Well, I wouldn't say *dangerous*, the doctor said. It's just, you know, rocks can grow.

Grow? the man said.

He'd never heard of that.

Grow, said the doctor. When you eat them, that is. Why, I once saw a woman with an eighty-pound boulder in her gut.

He shook his head.

It wasn't pretty, he said.

The man stared at the doctor.

So what do I do? he finally said.

It should probably come out, the doctor said.

OUT? said the man. You mean, surgery?

Do you really think that's necessary? he said.

The decision is yours, of course, said the doctor. But personally, I would recommend it.

THE man went home and thought about it. He told his wife what the doctor had said.

You should never have eaten that rock to begin with—what did you expect? she said.

THAT night, the man lay thinking about the rock. He could still feel it there, inside him. He could still feel its goodness radiating through him.

I don't want to lose the rock, he said.

SOME time went by. The doctor called.

I think I will keep the rock, the man said.

Are you sure? said the doctor.

Pretty sure, said the man.

Well, said the doctor, it's your decision. If you ever change your mind, though, let me know.

Okay, said the man.

And that was that.

~

MORE time went by. The man was happy. The rock felt good inside him.

But there was one thing that was bothering the man: The rock was definitely growing. The man's stomach was getting bigger and bigger. It was starting to stick out.

And the rock was getting heavier, too; the man was having a hard time standing up.

AND finally, one day, it got to the point where the man couldn't get out of bed.

So what? said his wife. You're just gonna lie there?

I can't move, said the man. What do you want?

This is all because of that dumb rock, his wife said. You should just get it cut out already.

I don't want it cut out, the man said. It's my rock. It's my rock; I ate it; it makes me happy.

THEN the pain set in. The rock had grown so big it was crowding out the man's innards.

You have to do it now, the man's wife said. You understand— you'll die if this keeps up.

The man knew that his wife was right. He could feel the rock filling up his body. He could still feel the goodness of it in there somewhere—but it was buried now beneath the pain and fear.

All right, the man said. Go get the doctor.

Finally, his wife said.

And she did.

THE surgery was hard. The doctor needed four men just to lift the rock out. They placed it on a scale, but the scale was crushed and the weight of the rock was never recorded.

Otherwise, everything went according to plan. They sewed the man's stomach back up. The doctor pronounced the procedure a success, and had a cigar on the porch.

TIME went by as the man recuperated. Then one day he woke up feeling fine. He patted his stomach and got out of bed, took a breath, and headed toward the door.

Where are you going? the man's wife said.

For a walk, said the man. I feel great!

THE man went out and walked and walked. It was a nice day and he felt the breeze and saw the clouds and heard the birds and everything was absolutely wonderful.

But after a while, the man started to feel different. He started to feel like something was wrong. He frowned and frowned, trying to figure it out, and then it hit him: It was the rock—the rock was gone! That was why he felt so hollow inside! There was a great big hole inside him!

And the man wiped his brow, and squinted, and squirmed.

And then the bad feeling got worse.

~

IN a panic, the man turned and ran to the field where he'd found the rock on that day so long ago. He looked around, all around, on the ground, everywhere, staring down, walking round in circles.

Another rock will make me feel good again, he thought. Another rock will be just what I need.

But he couldn't seem to find another rock like his. None of them looked right to him.

Oh, there were lots of other rocks, of course, but they were dull and brown and covered with dirt. None of them looked like the right one for him.

He ate some anyway, but they didn't work.

What am I going to do? the man said. How am I supposed to live like this?

And then it hit him, and he stopped and spun around.

My rock! Where is *my rock*? he said.

THE man ran frantically all the way home.

Where is the rock? he screamed.

What rock? said his wife.

The rock! screamed the man. The rock, the rock! My rock!

Oh, said his wife. It's out back. It was too heavy to carry very far.

THE man went out back. There it was—the rock!—over in the corner of the yard.

The man ran to it. He knelt down beside it.

He wrapped his arms around the stone.

He ran his hands all over its surface. He rubbed his face against it. It was way too big for him to eat, of course, but he held it, pressed it to his chest.

Oh rock! he said. How could I have been so stupid? And how can I get this empty feeling out?

And then the man heard a noise, and the rock cracked open.

And he stared into its dark and hungry mouth.

The End of the List

A WOMAN FINDS HERSELF standing in a maze. She frowns, looks this way and that. She turns and walks one way, goes around a corner, spins around, and suddenly finds herself in her kitchen.

Goodness, the woman says.

She puts a hand to her chest.

She steps into the dining room and looks around. She peers into the living room, then climbs up the stairs, goes in the bedroom, looks all around.

But there's no maze to be found in any of those places.

Well, says the woman. That was strange.

OVER dinner, the woman tells her husband what happened.

Should we go to a movie tonight? he says.

Okay, says the woman, after a while.

They finish their dessert in silence.

~

IN the theater, the two of them sit watching the movie. A group of Asian men are threatening each other with sticks.

The woman turns and looks all around.

I'll be right back, she says.

THE woman goes through the lobby, down the stairs toward the ladies' room. On the way, she sees a small door marked MAZE.

Oh, the woman says. That must be it!

And she opens the door and goes in.

THE woman wanders the maze for hours and hours. It actually turns out to be quite nice. It seems to be a hedge maze, but then, at other points, there are carpets and walls with fancy paintings.

The woman sits on a bench and stares up at the sky.

Through the blue, a plane is flying by.

Oh, says the woman. Well, look at that.

The plane moves off, leaving a line across the sky.

FOR some reason it is hard to get back to the theater. The woman swears she remembered the way, but now it seems different—plus the walls keep closing in, and thick vines keep trying to drag her the other way.

And then, when she does finally wind up in the theater, she finds herself trapped in the film.

The Asian men—who have now switched from sticks to knives—are screaming in a language she doesn't understand.

Harry! the woman keeps yelling into the audience. Harry, it's me! Get me out!

But despite all her yelling and banging on the screen, her husband keeps putting popcorn in his mouth.

THAT night the woman awakens with a start.

Oh God, she thinks. Oh my God!

She looks over and sees her husband lying beside her. He's asleep. His snoring is very loud.

FOR a moment, the woman lies there. Then she climbs out of bed and goes down to the kitchen and makes tea. She sits at the table, looks at her to-do list for tomorrow.

None of it looks very interesting.

THE woman gets a pen and sits there, thinking. She wants to add something to the list. She thinks and she thinks— and then she's got it.

Learn to fly, she writes.

And sets down the pen.

SHE heads back to bed, but then, halfway up the stairs, the woman suddenly pauses and turns. From its place way down at the foot of the stairs, the front door seems to be beckoning.

~

OUTSIDE, the night is chilly but clear. The moon is shining, and the hedges seem to glow.

The woman steps forward, stares up at the sky.

I guess, she says, tomorrow won't do.

She slips off her slippers, and sets them by the door, and then she takes a very deep breath. And she closes her eyes, and steps off the porch.

Oh, she says, as she feels a little lift.

The Man,
the Restaurant,
and the Eiffel Tower

THERE ONCE WAS a man who loved the Eiffel Tower. He loved it more than anything in the world. He had pictures of it up all over his walls, he had books about it, and little statues; he even had a recording he loved to listen to that consisted of various celebrities describing the first time they'd ever seen the Eiffel Tower.

Yet the man himself had never been to Paris.

WHY? Because the man had this restaurant. It had been in his family for generations. The man's father had run it, and his father before him, and now it was the man's turn, and he was worried.

He was worried that if he went away, the restaurant would go out of business. So he stayed there all day, every day, throughout the year.

And the Eiffel Tower never got his visit.

~

BUT then one day—it was on the morning of his fortieth birthday—the man found something on the kitchen table. It was a round-trip ticket in his name to Paris.

Surprise! said his children. Happy birthday!

BUT, said the man, I can't go to Paris! I can't go see the Eiffel Tower! You know I can't possibly leave the restaurant! I can't accept this—though really, I do appreciate it.

BUT then the man's children explained their whole plan. The man would take the plane to Paris, and they would stay home and run the restaurant.

Wasn't it the best birthday present ever?

BUT you don't know *how* to run a restaurant, the man said.

Of course we do, Dad, his children said. We've been watching you for years! We know everything! We know it all!

And finally, in the end, he was persuaded.

SO the man went to Paris, and had the time of his life. He climbed to the top of the Eiffel Tower. He stood there looking out at that beautiful skyline.

Wow! he kept saying, in his mind.

~

AND all the way home, the man thought about his children—how nice they were, how grand. How they'd turned out so well—how they loved him so much.

But when he arrived, he was in for a shock.

IT turned out the restaurant had gone completely under.

We're really sorry, Dad, his children said. We tried really hard! Really, we did! I guess we didn't know as much as we thought we did.

THE man was crushed. He thought about his father, and his father before him, and he cried. All those generations of working and slaving.

All that restauranteering down the drain.

BUT how could it even be possible? the man thought. How could it have happened like this?

The man stood and stared at the ground in confusion.

And what will I do now? he said.

SO the man went home and sat in his chair.

Can we get you anything, Dad? his children said.

No, said the man. I think I'll just sit here.

And sit there was just what he did.

~

BUT after a while, the man started to get bored of just sitting there, staring into space. He looked around a bit. He saw the pictures on the walls.

He saw the little statues on his shelves.

AND the man got up and put on his record of various celebrities talking about the Eiffel Tower.

Then he walked to the window and stood there, looking out.

And he thought about the skyline of Paris.

AND now, today, everything is fine. The man has a brand-new restaurant. It's not in the same town—or even the same country.

It's at the top of the Eiffel Tower.

IT's a beautiful little place, tasteful and clean. Romantically lit, and very cozy.

People come up hungry and go down full, a little tipsy, and always very happy.

ONE thing is the same—the celebrity recording. The man still plays it all day long. The only difference now is, the man talks along—or sings, rather, as though it were a song.

HIS children are there too—they work in the kitchen. On their breaks, they stand admiring the view.

Do you think we should tell Dad? they say to one another.

And finally, on Bastille Day, they do.

The Cracks
in the Sidewalks

THE CRACKS IN the sidewalks spell out people's names if you look at them from high-enough up. I first noticed this when I was up on the church steeple, doing a little carpentry work. Rebecca Stapleton was the first name I saw, down the sidewalk in front of town hall. And then Elsa Rice, out by the playground, and Terrence Ribbons by the grocery store.

I called a town meeting to ask people about it, but everyone was as surprised as me. We went up the ladder and stood on the church roof, a whole town silently staring down.

Rebecca Stapleton put a hand to her chest.

What does it mean? she said.

Terrence Ribbons was as white as a sheet.

Am I dreaming? Elsa Rice said.

~

WHAT about me? a voice piped up.

We turned; it was the Davis boy.

Is my name out there? he wanted to know.

He couldn't read. We all started to look.

We craned our necks, from all sides of the church; we found many other names, but not his.

After a while, he started to cry.

It's all right, we'll find it, I said.

I split the people up into a number of different groups, and we all started going roof to roof. The town is large, and pretty spread out; many sidewalks could only be seen from certain vantage points.

We found a whole slew of other names first, but then—finally—we found the boy's. It was all the way over on the far side of town, half-hidden behind the livery stable.

I stood beside the boy on the roof of the stable and helped him spell out his name on the ground. But then I heard the other voices calling.

Help me find *my* name! they were saying.

So I helped them search, and we found many more, but still there were a lot of names missing.

Then—suddenly—I had an idea.

Let's build a balloon, I said.

~

AND so we did. The ladies sewed fabric, and the men all built a wicker basket. And it wasn't long at all before we lifted off. I brought paper and pencil to map it out.

After three or four weeks, we'd found pretty much everyone, and everyone had their special place. Jonathan Edwards was by the grain silo; Mary Worth was in the alley behind the jail.

The only name missing at the very end was—by a strange stroke—my own. And, I have to tell you, it hit me pretty hard.

Where could it be? I said.

I'M sure it's not personal! the Levitts called up.

I'm sure it's out there somewhere! others said.

And so I kept the quest up—alone—for days. For days, and then for weeks and months.

I'd be up in the morning, wrestling with the basket, coiling the ropes, tending the fire; floating up one block and then down the next. Always, always staring down. But all I ever saw were other people's names—the same names, again and again.

At night I'd go home and lie in my bed.

Maybe go higher up, a voice said.

AND so I went higher, and then higher still, but I never caught sight of my name. And then, one day, the balloon wore out.

The fabric tore, and I came crashing down.

~

FOR weeks and weeks, I lay there in the hospital; the doctors said it was touch and go. When I finally got out, I looked like a skeleton.

They gave me a cane and a prescription to fill.

I walked toward downtown, and when I got there, I found everyone gathered in the square. There were lanterns and flags and a big pair of scissors.

They were having an opening ceremony.

IT turned out they'd built a replica of the town—the whole town, as seen from above. Every building, every street, every sidewalk was there.

I saw the names, chiseled in stone.

YOU'RE back! everyone said, when they saw me there. We're having a party; join in!

They brought me champagne and clapped me on the back. But I knew I didn't fit in.

AND so I slipped away, and went for a walk, just me alone with my cane. I tapped for a while over the names in the cracks. Then I stopped, and stepped off the walk.

I went veering off through the wild places—the tall grass, the alleys, the abandoned lots. I was looking for a hill, but there were none around; the land was flat for miles.

~

I was out in a field on the very edge of town, when my legs finally gave way. I tried to stop my fall with the cane, but it snapped, and I was on the ground.

I was lying there broken, just staring up, and then I started to cry.

Just for a moment, there in the clouds, I saw my own name go by.

Death and the Lady

A LADY GOES TO church one Sunday morning and notices Death sitting beside her in the pew.

Oh, Death! she says, very much surprised. Why, hello—I didn't see you!

Hello to you, too, miss, Death says with a smile. And what are we praying for today?

Oh, says the lady, long life—and happiness!

Ah, says Death. Sounds nice.

WHEN the service is over, the lady gets up to leave.

I'll see you later, Death, she says.

Indeed, says Death, I certainly hope so.

And he smiles and watches her walk away.

THE next week the lady returns to church, and Death is sitting there again.

Afternoon, miss, he says, with a smile.

If you don't mind, she says, I'm actually a ma'am.

Oh? says Death.

He looks a bit surprised.

I know, isn't it strange? the lady says.

She raises her hand and wiggles her wedding ring.

Well! says Death. Lucky man!

ARE you all right? the lady says, after a moment. You're looking a little pale, you know.

Working hard, says Death. Just working hard, is all.

Well, let's get some lunch, the lady says.

But . . . , says Death, motioning to the service.

Oh, don't worry about that, the lady says.

She rises from the pew and motions for Death to follow.

They have those all the time, she says.

THE lady takes Death to a nearby café. They sit at a table and eat bread and sausage.

Feel better? says the lady.

Oh yes, says Death. In fact, I do—very much!

For a moment, the two of them just sit there and smile.

Do you have any children? the lady says.

Oh no, says Death. Marriage is not for me. My career has to come first, you know.

I understand, the lady says, with her best understanding nod. I have a cousin like that. Wait, I think I have a picture in here.

She rummages around in her purse.

That's my husband, she says, passing Death a photo, and that's my sister, and my cousin. And that's my daughter, and those are the twins.

Handsome boys, says Death. You must be proud.

Just then a bell tolls in the distance.

Goodness, says the lady, I have to go! We're having a dinner party tonight and I still have so much to do.

Quite all right! says Death. I hope it goes well. And don't worry, I'll get the bill.

Are you sure? says the lady. I had a wonderful time.

Absolutely, says Death. I did too!

THE next week, the lady arrives at church to find Death sitting out front in a convertible.

I thought we might go for a drive, he says. After all, the weather's beautiful.

What a marvelous idea, the lady says, climbing in.

Is this yours? she says. The car?

Oh no, says Death. I took a vow of poverty. My uncle let me borrow it for the day.

Ah, says the lady. That's very nice of him! Well, on with it, Jeeves, let's go!

And Death laughs and puts the car into gear, and onward the two of them roll.

DEATH drives the lady up into the hills that stand overlooking the city. They park by a cliff and spread out a blanket and open up Death's picnic basket. They unpack a feast and lay it all out, and then they drink a toast.

To you, says Death.

No, you! says the lady.

Well then, says Death. To us both!

THE two lie on the blanket and laugh and talk. Death tells the lady about his job.

It's okay, he says. But sometimes I get lonely.

I know how you feel, the lady says.

You do? says Death. I always thought you were happy. Dinner parties and photographs and all.

Well, says the lady, things are different now. What with everyone gone.

Gone? says Death. But where did they go?

Well, my husband, you know, the lady says. And my daughter's married and in Sweden now, and the twins have moved to Maine.

Maine? Death says. But last week they were four.

Oh, that wasn't last week, the lady says. Maybe time moves differently for you. But I haven't seen you in ages.

But, says Death, gazing at her in awe. But you look exactly the same.

But even as he says that, he sees the old woman, like a ghost there moving beneath the skin.

Well, says Death.

He blinks and looks away.

You look the same to *me*, he says.

It's nice of you to say, the lady says, with a smile. And I still *feel* the same, on most days.

And what have *you* been up to? she suddenly says brightly, as if to change the subject.

Me? says Death. Oh well, not too much. Running up and down upon the earth.

Well tell me all about it, the lady says. I've never been anywhere in my life.

Nowhere? says Death.

Just here, the lady says. Is the rest of the world as nice?

Nice? Death says. I never thought of it that way. I like it best in Asia, I guess.

Did you see the Great Wall of China? the lady says.

Oh yes, says Death. Of course.

So he tells her about his time there, about the houses and the domes, about the sunsets and the spires. And he tells her about Egypt, and Iceland, and Norway, and Antarctica, and everywhere else.

It all sounds so nice, the lady says, with a sigh. I always meant to see the world, but there wasn't time.

Well, says Death, it's never too late. We can go—and if you want, you can drive.

He raises a hand and motions to the car.

Oh, I couldn't, the lady says. And besides, don't you have a job to be at?

I could take some time off, Death says.

The lady looks at Death and Death looks back. Then, with a smile, she starts to nod.

All right, she says, you got yourself a deal. Now please, help an old lady up.

So Death stands up and takes the lady's arm, and he walks her slowly to the car. He helps her in and then climbs in himself. She turns the key and the engine roars.

Okay now, says Death. Are you sure you want to do this?

I do, says the lady. But first, a kiss.

So Death leans in, and they close their eyes.

And they kiss.

Then she floors it off the cliff.

Spiders

THE CITY IS in the midst of an epidemic—giant spiders are everywhere. The man hears about it on the news, sitting alone in his apartment.

Oh, leave the giant spiders alone, he says.

Live and let live—that's his motto.

BUT that night when the man goes out for a walk, he is attacked by a giant spider. It rolls him up into a sticky cocoon and drags him down an alley to its web.

Let me go! yells the man. Let me go, let me go!

It's no use fighting, a voice says.

The man looks over. There's a woman beside him, wrapped in a cocoon just like his.

Who're you? says the man.

My name's Lois, the woman says.

It's nice to meet you, she adds.

Likewise, says the man. How long have you been here?

Oh, about an hour, the woman says. It's hard to be sure because I can't see my watch. But, about an hour, I'd say.

How are we going to get out of this? the man says.

Oh, I don't think we will! the woman says. I've already screamed myself hoarse, you see, and there's no way to break these silken threads.

The man tries his own bindings to be sure.

They *are* extremely strong, he says.

He'll probably be back to eat us pretty soon—he certainly is voracious! the woman says.

Eat us? says the man.

Of course, the woman says. What do you think spiders do with their prey?

I don't know, says the man. I never thought about it.

Well you might want to start, the woman says.

The man looks over at her. He tilts his head.

How'd you get here, anyway? he says.

Well, says the woman, I was out walking little Kneehigh—Kneehigh's my dog, you know—when this great big spider just swept down and grabbed me. And here I am.

That's awful, the man says.

Yes, says the woman. But at least Kneehigh got away. I don't know what I'd have done if he'd been eaten. Probably would've died right then and there on the spot.

The man makes his best understanding face.

And you? says the woman. Do you have any pets?

No, says the man. I'm a bachelor.

Bachelors can still have pets, the woman says.

I know, says the man. But I don't.

Well, says the woman, really, you should. Pets just make you feel so much better.

They do? says the man.

Oh yes! says the woman. Why, Little Kneehigh is my *raison d'être*.

That's French, she says. It means *reason for being*.

I always wondered what that meant, the man says.

Just then the giant spider reappears and comes running toward them down the alley.

Aaaaaah! screams the woman, as the spider lunges at her.

Leave her alone! the man yells.

But the giant spider does not leave her alone. Instead, it sinks its teeth into her neck. It sinks its teeth in and sucks all the blood out of Lois's body.

And then it runs away again.

THE man lies there in the web—petrified. He stares at Lois's dead, shriveled body.

Lois? he says. Lois? Lois? Lois, are you all right? Lois?

But Lois doesn't answer, doesn't say a word, doesn't even make a single move. And, eventually, the man starts to cry.

Then he starts thinking, to push the tears away.

In his mind, the man envisions powerful weapons. He envisions guns and knives and hand grenades. He envisions nets and sharp sticks, crossbows, bows and arrows. He envisions himself taking many spiders' lives.

But then the man frowns—he's suddenly noticed that the threads binding his body have been cut.

The spider must have brushed against me, he thinks, with its bristles, during its exit.

The man untangles himself from the cocoon. It's slow going, but he gets it done. He tears free of the web and drops to the ground. He looks back up at Lois's body.

I'll get them, Lois! he says. I swear I will! For you! I'll kill every single one of them!

HE moves off down the alley. He peers into the street. No sign of the giant spiders.

Gun store's that way, he says, and moves into the night.

But then he hears a sound—a bark.

He looks and sees a small dog on the pavement.

The dog is wearing a collar. The collar, in turn, is attached to a leash. The leash is leading off to nowhere.

Kneehigh? says the man. Are you Lois's little Kneehigh?

The dog sticks its tongue out and pants. The man kneels down and pats it on the head. He reaches for the name tag on the collar.

Kneehigh, the man reads. So it *is* you.

Kneehigh blinks up at the man. The man suddenly smiles. The smile just happens, rises up from somewhere down inside.

Now what are we going to do with *you?* the man says.

For a moment, he thinks about the spiders. He thinks

about the guns, the knives and hand grenades, the destruction he wanted to wreak, the slaughter.

Then he picks up Kneehigh's leash and starts to lead him home.

Come on, he says. Let's go.

They stop at a phone booth and call the police.

And then they continue on home.

THE man puts a blanket for Kneehigh on the couch. Then he fills a bowl with some water. They split a hamburger he finds in the fridge, and sit down before the TV together.

Oh, the man says, when the news comes on.

It's all about the war against the spiders.

Well, he says. Don't have to watch that!

He finds *Jeopardy!*, and holds Kneehigh even tighter.

The Sloth

A BUNCH OF SLOTHS were hanging out, eating leaves in the forest, when one of them suddenly spoke up.

Hey guys, he said. I think I'm gonna get a job.

Gonna get a what? another said.

A job, said the sloth. You know, something to do. Don't you guys ever get tired of eating leaves?

But nobody answered.

And finally, the sloth sighed.

I guess I'll see you later, he said.

THE sloth crawled down from the tree and headed off— very, very slowly—through the forest.

He came to some ants building an anthill.

You guys need any help? he said.

The ants didn't answer; they just ran around in circles.

I'm looking for a job, the sloth said.

But the ants just looked really confused and upset.

I'm sorry, the sloth said. Never mind.

THE sloth crawled on, until he came to a bear who was reaching into a beehive for some honey.

Excuse me, said the sloth, do you need help with that?

This is mine! the bear roared. *My honey!*

OKAY, said the sloth.

He slowly backed away.

Next, he came to a stream. And on it, he saw some beavers building a dam.

You guys need help with that? he said.

What's that? said the head beaver, who was wearing a hard hat.

I'm looking for a job, the sloth said.

Sorry, said the beaver. This here's a union shop.

But maybe try the city? he added.

The city! said the sloth.

He'd never thought of that.

And which way would that be? he said.

Oh, said the beaver, just pick a direction!

So the sloth did exactly that.

THE city turned out to be not so far away, which was good, because the sloth traveled *slow*. And by the time he got there, he was absolutely famished.

What I need, he said, is some food.

~

HE crawled all through the city, up and down the streets, looking for leaves to eat. But there were no leaves—in fact, there were no trees!

I'm so hungry, I could die, the sloth said.

A passerby heard him and pointed down the block.

There's a soup kitchen down that way, she said.

Soup? said the sloth.

He didn't know what that was.

It turned out it wasn't so great.

PEOPLE eat this stuff? the sloth asked the others who were sitting at the table in the shelter.

Well, one of them said, the thing is, it's free.

When I get a job, said the sloth, I'll eat better.

So the next day, the sloth got up bright and early and crawled off down the street to look around. Every now and then, he'd see a HELP WANTED sign, and then he'd comb his hair and crawl in.

I'M here about the job, the sloth would always say.

And the people would always look at him the same.

The job? they'd say. Aren't you a sloth?

A sloth who wants to work, the sloth would say.

~

AND usually the people would just wave him off, but sometimes they'd give him a shot.

Here, type this letter up, for instance, they'd say. Or, give this car an oil change, to start.

AND the sloth would do his best—he'd try very hard—but the fact was, he was just *very slow*. And then, on top of that, of course, he didn't have hands—basically, the sloth was all toes.

WHAT'S this? the people would say, after he'd typed up the letter, as they stared at the mess upon the page.

Or, Why'd you pour the oil all over yourself?

Or, Pizza's supposed to be *circular*!

IT was all very trying, and at the end of the day, the sloth went and crawled back to the shelter, and he sat there and looked at his meager bowl of soup.

Well, he said, I'll try again tomorrow.

AND try again he did—the next day and the next. And then, for some weeks and months. He never got a job—in fact, he never came close—but he never once thought about giving up.

NOT, of course, that that did him any good—he was steadfast, but he was still eating soup.

And then, one night, the sloth just cracked.

He started sobbing so hard he dropped his spoon.

WELL, what's the matter? his tablemates all said—he'd always been such a sturdy sloth.

It's just so incredibly discouraging! the sloth said. I'm a good sloth! And all I want is a job!

OH hey, the people said, hey, it's not your fault—the job market's impossible in this town!

Is it? said the sloth, wiping his eyes. I thought it was just me who couldn't get one!

OH no—look at me! one of them said. I haven't had a job in months! I've got eighteen years' experience driving a truck—but there's just no work for truck drivers around!

No? said the sloth.

He thought for a moment.

Could you drive a Zamboni? he said.

A Zamboni? said the truck driver. Like at an ice skating rink?

Yeah, said the sloth. 'Cause that job's available.

IS it? said the truck driver, and his eyes got very wide. Where is the ice skating rink?

It's on Elm Street, said the sloth. Behind the municipal building. I think they're open until eight.

~

Eight? said the truck driver.

He quickly checked his watch. Then he got up and ran out of the room.

Everyone else just sat there a moment.

Well, what about me? a woman said.

What about you? said the sloth. What can you do?

I used to be a teacher, she said. But then the whole school system downsized overnight, and now there's no teaching jobs anywhere.

Hmm, said the sloth. You have a great voice. Have you thought about a career in radio?

Radio? said the woman, suddenly smiling. Oh no! But, well, of course, I'd love to!

Well, said the sloth, go down to KPPD and talk to Jeremy in the front office. They're looking for someone to do educational reporting. I failed to get that job this morning.

And the sloth went down the table, to each person, one by one, and he matched them all up with available jobs. And each of them smiled and then got up from the table and went out the door at a run.

Until finally, it was just the sloth, sitting there alone—all alone with his bowl of soup.

He looked at it awhile and then picked up his spoon.

He slurped it quietly, there in the empty room.

BUT then, one by one, the people came back—and all of them were laughing and smiling.

I got it! they all said. I got it—I got the job!

And they hugged the sloth—and put money in his hand.

WHAT's this? said the sloth.

It's money! the people said. It's for you! I can't thank you enough!

Really? said the sloth, looking down at the money. I don't think I did very much.

BUT later that night—when the dancing was over—the sloth mulled it over in bed.

And in the morning, he didn't go out and look for a job—he opened an employment agency instead.

PEOPLE came in, and the sloth sat there with them, and he figured out what they were good at. And then he matched those qualities up in his mind with the job openings he was aware of.

AND with the money he made, the sloth found an apartment— nothing fancy, just one with lots of light. And he filled it completely full—floor to ceiling, wall to wall—with potted plants and trees of every height.

Not bad, he said, smiling, and he put in a stereo, strung up a hammock between the trees.

Then he invited his friends to his housewarming party.

Thanks for coming! he said. Please, try the leaves.

The Ostrich
and the Aliens

THE OSTRICH IS standing with its head in the sand when it becomes aware of a high-pitched noise. It looks up to see a large spherical object come in for a landing nearby.

The ostrich watches as it settles to the ground. Then it wanders over for a closer look.

The object is silver, and very, very shiny.

It doesn't smell particularly good.

THE ostrich taps on the thing with its beak.

A door opens and an alien looks out.

Yeah, it's definitely a life form, it says to the second alien inside.

Well, ask it! says the second. Bring it on in!

The first alien extends a ramp.

Come on up! he says.

He waves for the ostrich.

The ostrich walks up the ramp into the ship.

~

WELCOME, says the alien. We're hoping you can help us. We're trying to find the Promised Land.

The ostrich blinks. It stares at the alien.

Do you know where it is? says the other alien.

The ostrich looks around at the saucer's blinking lights. It reaches out and pecks the steering console.

No! says the second alien. Don't touch that, please! Those are extremely important!

HERE, says the alien. We have this map.

He spreads it out on the floor.

We're here, he says. But where's the Promised Land?

The ostrich turns and looks out the door.

NO, here, says the alien.

He taps on the map.

The ostrich goes over and looks at it.

Then it turns around and runs back down the ramp and sticks its head into the sand.

THE aliens stand there, staring down at it.

I'm not sure he's very intelligent, the second says.

He does seem a little strange, says the first. But perhaps it's just the language barrier.

~

THE two walk down the ramp and stand by the ostrich.

The ostrich lifts its head out of the sand. It blinks at the aliens, sticks its head back in.

Now come on, the first alien says. We're strangers here, you know—be a good guide.

Yeah, the second alien says. There's something wrong—our charts don't work! And our boss said we have to find the Promised Land!

THE ostrich suddenly makes a strange, strangled sound. It lifts its head out of the sand.

It starts to run away.

Then it glances back.

I think it wants us to follow, the alien says.

ALL right, says the second, and the two of them take off—on their tentacles, scurrying across the sand.

The ostrich leads them across the desert for miles.

The creature's legs are very long! the alien says.

YEAH, says the second, who's starting to gasp. My tentacles weren't designed for this!

Mine neither! says the first. And this place is a nightmare—who'd imagine a whole planet made of dirt?

~

JUST then, up ahead, the ostrich stops.

Both aliens collapse in the sand.

Hey, what's that? the first alien says.

There's a strange shape ahead on the horizon.

THE two aliens lie there, staring over at it.

Is it the Promised Land? the first alien says.

No, says the second, after a minute. No, it isn't.

It's their flying saucer.

SHIT, says the first alien.

They both look at the ostrich.

The ostrich stares back at them. It blinks.

You're a very stupid animal, the alien says. I hope you're happy with yourself.

I don't know, says the second. Maybe there's something more.

Something more? says the first. Like what?

Maybe it's a parable, the second alien says. Or, you know, like, a metaphor.

I don't get it, says the first.

Yeah, me neither, says the second. But let's just think on it a bit.

They walk toward the ship.

They stand there a minute.

Then they look down at their feet.

You don't think . . . ? says the first.

The second shakes his head.

I don't think, but it's possible, he says. Maybe there was a great big sandstorm or something and the Promised Land was buried underneath?

THEY look at the ostrich.

The ostrich stares back. It looks from one alien to the other.

It looks at the ground.

Then up at the aliens.

Then down at the ground again.

WELL, says the first alien. Who's going first?

I'm not doing this alone, the second says.

Fine, says the first, we'll do it together.

And together they lower their heads.

THE ostrich waits until their heads are in the sand, and then, abruptly, it lays an egg.

Then it walks up the ramp and into the ship, and it closes the hatch and flies away.

The Madman

THE MADMAN CAME stumbling into the town. He was dehydrated, delirious; he couldn't speak. Who knows how long he'd been out there in the desert?

So we took pity on him and took him in.

We nursed him and fed him and stayed with him through the nights, until finally, he came back to health. But when he started to talk, we were all somewhat shocked.

He spoke only of the Armies of Hell.

THE madman described them in full, vivid detail, as he stared into his mind with open eyes. Giant dragons, winged specters, snakes with many heads. Women with scissors for legs.

At first, we dismissed it—we tried to laugh it off.

The man's been through a lot, we said.

But as the days went by, his talk never stopped.

He spoke only of the Armies of Hell.

~

Now please, sir, we told him, let's talk of other things.

We asked him about his life, where he was from.

But the madman ignored us—it was like we weren't there. He spoke only of the Armies of Hell.

He spoke of crawling mouths, of trees with blood-filled eyes. He spoke of clouds made of poison and spikes. He spoke of werewolves and gorgons, vampires and zombies, babies that would eat you from inside.

And as the madman ranted on, his voice grew very loud, until finally he was screaming at the top of his lungs. We tried to calm him, to help him—we gave him peaceful drugs. But nothing worked; he just raved and ranted on.

And he didn't rant for just an hour, or only during the day—he ranted and screamed all night long. There was no way to get away; our village was small.

And our nights then became very long.

We'd lie there in the dark, listening to the madman yelling and screaming those awful things. And we couldn't help but picture them, the demons he described. We couldn't take it—they were in us, in our dreams.

At first we tried to kick him out. We brought him sacks of food, shoes and clothes to wear, full waterskins. We took him to the edge of town and gently pushed him out.

Time to move on now, we said.

But did the madman leave us? No! He came back. So we

turned him around and tried again. We begged him and we pleaded; we even gave him gold.

But the madman came back—and back again.

So finally, of course—and we're not proud of this—finally, we pelted him with stones. We didn't mean to hurt him—at first, they were merely warnings. But he ignored them—until one broke his nose.

And when that first rock broke his nose, and the blood came spurting out, finally something changed—you could see. Something in his eyes—as if they'd finally focused. As if, for the first time, he could see.

And in that same moment, the madman stopped ranting. And he looked at us, and fell to his knees.

And he raised up his arms, and I think he mouthed a word.

I don't know, but it might have been *Please*.

The Porpoise

A MAN GETS A job working for the circus. The whole thing happens very fast: He's sitting in his house, he's unhappy with his life, then he picks up the paper and sees an ad.

THE CIRCUS IS COMING! the ad says in big letters. DON'T YOU WANT TO WORK FOR THE CIRCUS?

Hmm, says the man.

He puts down the paper.

Then he walks out the door and starts the car.

THE man drives downtown to where they're setting the tent up. He gets out of the car and looks around.

Hey, he says, to a guy sitting behind a table. Is this where you get the circus jobs?

Yeah, says the guy—he looks like the ringmaster. But the thing is, we only have one left.

Oh? says the man. And which one is that?

Swimming with the porpoises, the guy says.

~

PORPOISES? says the man. I didn't even know you had those. I thought the circus was just tigers and stuff.

Nope, says the guy, we got porpoises, too. So what do you say—you want the job?

OKAY, says the man.

Great, says the guy. Sign this form. And initial it here.

The man takes the pen and makes the required marks.

Welcome aboard! says the guy. You start tomorrow.

TOMORROW? says the man. That doesn't leave me much time.

What do you need time for? the guy says.

Well, says the man.

He thinks for a minute.

Be here seven a.m. sharp, says the guy.

THE man drives on home. He's feeling a little grumpy.

What's all the rush? he says. I mean, what if I had something important to do tomorrow?

He drinks a beer, watches TV, and goes to bed.

ALMOST immediately, the man has a dream. In his dream, he's in the water with a porpoise.

With a shock, the man sits bolt upright in bed.

But I don't know how to swim! he says.

~

SOMEHOW this fact had eluded him before.

I'm sure the circus'll train me, he says.

But maybe they won't, he says a minute later. What if they just assumed?

THE man throws the sheet back.

I'm gonna drown! he says. I mean, it's right there in the job title—I have to swim!

He gets up and paces back and forth about the room.

I need swimming lessons! he says.

THE man finds the phone book and picks up the phone. He calls the local YMCA. He gets a recording all about swimming lessons. They start the week after next.

But I could be dead by then! the man says in a panic. I have to learn how to swim tonight!

Think, think! he says, and thinks hard.

Suddenly he thinks of Sally Rhinehardt.

THE man hasn't thought of Sally Rhinehardt in years. She was the man's high school girlfriend. He broke up with her a few days after graduation.

Jeez, that was dumb of me, he thinks.

Hmm, says the man.

He looks at the phone.

Sally Rhinehardt was the state swimming champion. She

had come *this close* to making it to the Olympics. It had been like dating a fish woman.

THE man picks the phone up and dials Sally's number—twenty years, and he still knows it by heart.

Hello? says a voice.

Sally? says the man.

Luke? Sally says. Luke Deveraux?

THE man gets in his car and drives to Sally's house. When he gets there, it's after one a.m. But Sally's got the backyard pool all heated and lit up.

Thanks so much for doing this, he says.

No problem, Sally says. Come on down into the water.

It's good to see you again, she adds.

You too, says the man, feeling awkward in his trunks.

All right, Sally says, you start like this.

THE man stays in the pool with Sally for hours.

You're a very fast learner! she says.

The man does the breast stroke up and down the pool.

Then he stops and kisses Sally.

She kisses back.

OH, Luke, Sally says. I'm so glad you called.

I'm so glad you answered, he says.

They hold each other close.

Then they climb out of the pool, and towel off, and run in to bed.

AT about seven a.m., the man suddenly laughs.

I'm supposed to be at the circus, he says.

Oh, Sally says. Are you still going to go?

What? the man says. Hell no!

BUT just at that moment, there's a knock on the door. More like a pounding—a banging!

The two of them leap up and jump out of bed.

Who could that be? they say.

CIRCUS! blares a voice through a megaphone from outside. Come on out, we know you're in there, Luke Deveraux!

The man leans over and peers out through the blinds.

I don't want to go! he says. I changed my mind!

BUT the guy with the bullhorn holds up a piece of paper.

You signed a contract! he says. You can't get out of it! It's legal—ironclad!

And the police are here to enforce it! he adds.

SURE enough, behind the guy—and the clowns—there are policemen. They're all holding billy clubs in their hands.

Shit! says the man.

He looks at Sally in fear.

Hurry, come with me! she says.

SALLY leads the man out through the kitchen door, down the spiral stairs, into the secret garage.

Get in, Sally says, motioning to the dune buggy.

The garage door opens, and the giant engine roars.

THEY squeal off over the hills. Behind, the sirens whine. The clowns are shaking their fists from their tiny car.

You can't get away! yells the guy with the megaphone. You can't avoid the circus *and* the law!

THE man is still terrified—but Sally's jaw is set.

The hell with those jokers, she says.

She spins the wheel hard. The buggy leaps forward and crashes through the doors of a shopping mall.

THEY speed past the shops, leap the central fountain, and crash out through the back wall of a Spencer's Gifts. And then they speed away, across the parking lot—

But the cops and the circus are right behind.

THEY come up over a rise and Sally slams on the brakes.

They jump out—they're at the edge of a cliff.

The man looks at Sally. She reaches for his hand.

Come on, count of three! she says.

~

THE two leap from the cliff as their pursuers arrive.
    They splash down into the water and bob back up.
    The clowns and the cops stand glaring from the cliff.
    You can't get away! the ringmaster yells.

BUT get away they can—and get away they do! They swim
away from the shore in perfect form. The figures on the cliff
top grow smaller and smaller, until they can't even see them
anymore.

I'M sorry I broke up with you after high school! the man
says. I don't know what I could possibly have been thinking!
    It's all right! Sally says. I had a lot to learn! For some
reason, I was really wrapped up in swimming!

AND the two of them laugh and they swim out together,
while behind them, the land fades away.
    And finally they come to Sally's secret boat.
    It's named *The Porpoise*.
    And on *The Porpoise*, they sail away.

III.

The Dragon

A FAMILY GOES ON a day trip to Chinatown, and the next morning, the little girl finds a dragon in their backyard.

Are you a dragon? the little girl says to the dragon.

Yes, says the dragon. I am.

The dragon is swaying a bit from side to side.

What are you doing here? says the girl.

I came to play, says the dragon. That is, unless you'd rather keep playing alone?

The little girl looks at the dragon and thinks, and then, finally, she shakes her head.

No, she says to the dragon, it's okay.

And she and the dragon start to play.

THAT night, the little girl is getting ready for bed.

Did you see the dragon? she asks her mom.

The dragon? says her mother. You mean, in Chinatown?

Today! says the girl. In the yard!

Oh, says her mom, drawing the sheet back. No, I didn't know it was there.

It was, says the girl. We played ring-around-the-rosy, and house. And hide-and-seek—twice.

And was the dragon a nice dragon? her mom says after a while.

A nice dragon? the little girl says.

He didn't say anything frightening? says her mom.

Of course not, says the girl. He's a dragon!

Well that's good, her mom says. Okay, it's time for bed. But first, you have to make me a promise.

A promise? says the girl.

Yes, says her mom. You have to promise me this: If the dragon ever says or does anything bad, anything mean, or that you think is wrong, you will come tell me—immediately. All right?

All right, says the little girl. I promise.

Good, says her mom.

And the girl gets in bed, and the two of them kiss each other good night. Then the mom stands up and leaves the room.

And everything is all right.

But later that night, as the girl lies in bed—thinking it over—she starts to frown. She can't understand why her mom would say those things about the dragon.

I'll have to ask him, she says.

~

I have no idea, the dragon says the next day. You sure she didn't say anything else?

That's all she said, the little girl says.

But what could *I* do wrong? the dragon says.

I don't know, says the girl. That's what I asked.

Well, what about your father? the dragon says. What did *he* have to say about all this?

He wasn't there, the girl says. So I didn't ask.

Well, says the dragon. Don't you think you should?

The girl thinks.

You think so? she says.

She looks at the dragon.

Why don't *you* ask him? she says.

I'm not allowed in the house, the dragon says.

THAT night the little girl goes to see her father.

Do you think the dragon is bad? she says.

The dragon? says her father.

She has an imaginary friend, her mother says (she's sitting beside him on the couch).

He's a dragon, she adds. From when we went to Chinatown.

Ah, says the father. Of course.

He looks at the girl. He thinks for a moment.

Do *you* think the dragon's bad? he says.

No, says the little girl. I don't think so.

Then I don't think so either, the father says.

Then why isn't he allowed in the house? says the girl.

The mom and dad look at each other.

Who said he's not allowed in the house? the dad says.

He did, says the girl. The dragon.

The dragon said that? the mother says, and the girl nods.

The mom and dad get up and leave the room.

WE don't think you should play with the dragon quite so much, the parents say when they come back into the room.

What? says the little girl. Why not?

We just think it would be better, her parents say.

Is he a bad dragon? the little girl says.

Oh no! says the girl's mom. Not at all! It's just—the truth is, he doesn't even exist! He's just made up, but now he's becoming too real.

You think I made up the dragon? the girl says.

Yes, honey, her mom says. We do.

But why? says the girl. Why do you think that?

Honey, says her dad. Dragons aren't real.

THE next day the little girl is playing in the yard when the dragon comes around the fence. The little girl sees him but she tries to ignore him.

What's the matter? the dragon finally says.

Nothing, says the girl. But I'm not supposed to talk to you.

What did I do *now*? the dragon says.

Nothing, says the girl, shaking her head. It's just, you don't really exist.

Don't exist? says the dragon. What do you mean?

I mean you're just made up, says the girl. I made you up. You're not a real dragon.

I am too, the dragon says.

No you're not, says the girl.

Watch this, the dragon says, and he flies all around the yard—from one end to the other, and then back again.

You're still not really real, says the girl.

What about this? the dragon says. And he blows a plume of fire across the yard. It burns away a small tree in the corner.

You can't do that! says the girl. You're not real!

The dragon stands there and stares at the girl.

Well, he says, if I'm not really real, then how come I'm not allowed in the house? What kind of sense does *that* make? None at all!

The little girl frowns. She looks at the ground.

Your parents are just *mean people*, the dragon says. They just don't want you to have friends besides them. *That's* why I'm not allowed in the house.

Even if that's true, the little girl says, what can I do? I'm just a girl!

And the two of them stand there in silence awhile.

I might have an idea, the dragon says.

The little girl looks up. She wipes away a tear.

Well, what is it? she says.

Well, says the dragon, I can make myself really small.

Really? You can do that? says the girl.

Yes, says the dragon. I can. It's true—it's a talent all us dragons have. So what we'll do is, I'll shrink myself way, way down, and then you open your mouth.

My mouth? says the girl, and makes a face.

Don't worry, it's not gross, the dragon says. When I'm that small, I don't even taste like anything! I'll just fly right down into your stomach. And then I'll be in there, and no one will know, and we can do anything we want!

You'd live in my stomach? the little girl says.

Yes, says the dragon. Or thereabouts.

But would we still get to play? the girl says.

Of course, says the dragon. All the time! In fact, we'd get to play *even more*, because I'd be right there with you, inside!

Really? says the girl.

Then suddenly she frowns.

But would it be a bad thing? she says.

Oh no! says the dragon. It would be great! It would be the best thing in the world!

THAT evening when the mother comes to call the girl in, she finds her sitting alone at the picnic table.

Time to come in, the mother says. Dinner's ready.

Oh, okay, says the girl.

No dragon today? her mom says, looking around.

No, says the girl, he's gone. And besides, you know, he wasn't really real.

I'm glad to hear you say that, says her mom.

~

AND the little girl stands and takes her mother's hand, and the two of them head back into the house. But just before the girl takes that first step over the threshold, she stops for a moment and looks down.

Everything okay? says her mom.

But the girl doesn't answer.

Then she takes a very deep breath.

And she steps inside and stands there a moment.

Then she grins.

Oh yes, she says.

The Candelabra

THE GRANDMOTHER STARTS staying up later and later, long after everyone else has gone to bed. She sits in the living room, quietly, in the dark, with her hands folded in her lap.

One night the mother—her daughter—finds her there. She's on her way to the bathroom.

Mother, she says, what are you doing? She reaches out and turns on the light.

Don't, says the grandmother. She holds up a hand.

But what are you doing? the mother says.

She waits for an answer, but no answer comes.

You can't just sit here in the dark, she says.

THE next morning, the grandmother gets up early and goes out for a walk.

She looks through the shops that line the street.

In one of them, she finds a candelabra.

How much is this? she asks the shopkeeper.

That old thing? he says.

He names a price.

I'll take it, she says.

He wraps it up and hands her the bag.

THE grandmother goes home and puts the candelabra in the closet. Late that night, she sets it up. She puts in the candles, one by one, when everyone else is fast asleep.

She strikes a match to light the candles, but just then the mother appears.

Oh! she says.

She rushes forward.

You'll burn the whole house down! she says.

The grandmother sighs. She blows out the match. She sets it down on a tray.

I'm sorry, she says.

She takes out the candles.

What's gotten into you? the mother says.

THE next morning, the grandmother doesn't get out of bed. Instead, she lies there, staring at the wall.

Somewhere around noon, the mother looks in.

Are you feeling all right? she says.

The grandmother nods, but doesn't say a word.

The mother stands there for a while. Then she turns and walks off down the hall.

That day, the grandmother passes on.

~

THE family is stricken. They arrange the funeral. They put on their mourning clothes. They go and stand and watch as the grandmother is lowered into the ground.

For weeks afterward, they don't know what to do. They get dressed, go to work, come home.

One night the mother decides they should put things away, clean out the grandmother's room.

THEY go into her room and start to clean. They look through photo books, old clothes. They handle the jewelry and leaf through old letters.

They find the candelabra in the closet.

THEY take it to the living room and set it up. They put all the candles in. Then they find the matches, and light the candles, very slowly, one by one.

THEY sit in the dim light, all together.

Not one of them says a word.

And they watch as the shadows dance upon the walls.

And for a while, the grandmother's returned.

The Fall

WHEN THE MAN comes to, he's at the top of a cliff, and the woman is falling down. He reaches out instinctively and tries to grab her, but it's far too late for that now.

He closes his eyes as she hits the rocks below, and winces at the sickening sound. When he looks again, a pool of blood is forming.

He finds a staircase and makes his way down.

AT the bottom, he approaches and stands by the body. Her blood touches his shoe; he steps back. He peers at her face. It's half torn away.

He has no idea who she is.

AFTER a while, the man turns away. He makes his way back up to the road. There's no car, no people; he doesn't know where he is.

He starts walking, and eventually gets to town.

~

HE finds the police station and tells a cop the story. The cop drives him back out to the scene. But when they get there and stand looking down from the cliff, there's nothing there—nothing at all to be seen.

I don't understand, the man says. She was there.

They walk down the stairs and look around.

You have to believe me—*it happened*, says the man.

But there's no blood; even his shoe is now clean.

THE cop drives the man back to the police station.

You'll have to fill out some forms, he says.

The man does, and as he does, he starts to remember—his name, where he lives, his job.

THE man goes home and returns to his life. For a while it all seems like a dream. He goes to work, comes home; he sits, he eats dinner.

And in time, it becomes real to him.

THEN one day on the street, the man passes a woman. But not just *a* woman—*the* woman! It's her!

Wait! the man says.

He turns as she passes.

The woman looks at him—and her eyes widen in fear.

~

IT'S you! the man says, but the woman moves away.

He hurries after her; in response, she starts to run. The man runs faster—he reaches out, grabs her arm.

Then from nowhere, the cop's hand grabs his own.

THE cop takes the two of them down to the police station. The man sits on a bench in the lobby. Through a window, he watches as the cop interviews the woman.

But he can't hear or make out what they say.

WHEN the interview's done, the cop opens the door and watches as the woman walks away. She gives a fearful glance at the man on the bench.

Go on home, ma'am, the cop says. It's all right.

THE man rises from the bench. The cop stops him with a hand.

Where's she going? the man says. What'd she say?

She said nothing, says the cop. Because nothing happened. Just forget it. Just leave her alone.

THE man tries to argue, tries to get more from the cop, but the cop has nothing more to say.

Just go home, he says.

The man leaves the police station.

Then he slips into a shadowy doorway.

~

THAT night when the cop leaves, the man follows after him. He follows him all the way to his home. He stands outside, watches the cop through a window.

He follows him like that every night.

AND one night, the cop doesn't go home after work. Instead, he emerges well dressed. He drives to a house way out on the edge of town.

He rings the doorbell, and the woman opens up.

THE cop and the woman go out to dinner. The man follows them and watches from a distance. He can't hear their words, but their smiles say a lot.

They go out again and again.

ONE night the two of them go for a long drive. The man tails them discreetly in his car. They wend their way back in a familiar direction.

They stop by the cliff where the woman fell.

THE man watches as the two of them walk to the cliff and stand looking down at the rocks. The cop motions to the stairs and they start to climb down.

Soon, they are out of the man's sight.

~

THE man turns the engine off and climbs out of the car. He approaches the edge of the cliff. He stands and looks down, and there on the rocks below, he sees the cop and the woman making love.

FOR a moment, the man stands, just watching them move. Then his foot seems to slip, and he falls.

The pair look up as he comes rushing down.

His arms are wide enough to hold them all.

Fernando

A MAN AWAKENS ONE morning to find that he has forgotten his name. He lies in bed, staring at the ceiling.

Biff? he thinks. Ted?

He looks around the room.

Harold? he thinks. Harold? Is my name Harold?

THE man goes into the kitchen and pours a bowl of cereal.

Joe? he thinks. Is it Joseph?

But a moment later, he shakes his head.

Nope, he thinks. Not Joseph.

He looks around.

There must be something in this house that has my name on it, he says.

HOURS later, he's searched the whole house.

His name is nowhere to be found.

~

THE man goes next door and knocks on his neighbor's door.

What's my name? he says when his neighbor answers.

I don't know, says his neighbor. I don't think you ever told me. In fact, I've never seen you before.

THE man decides to stop thinking about it. Instead, he goes to work. He drives to the office and sits at his desk. He looks around at the various other employees.

They all have little nameplates on their desks with their names engraved on them.

The man looks at his own desk.

He has no nameplate.

I have to get a name, the man says.

ON the way home from work, the man stops at the bookstore. He buys a book of names and goes home.

Herman, reads the man. Lionel. Aloysius.

None of the names sound right.

The man keeps reading.

Franklin, he reads. Francis. Frederick. Fernando.

The man stops. He looks up and thinks.

He kind of likes Fernando.

THE next day when the man goes to work he is whistling a little tune.

My name is Fernando, he says to the office.

Everyone looks at him, but no one says a word.

Fernando, the man says again, a little louder this time. My name is Fernando.

Nothing.

THE man goes into his office and sits in his chair. He picks up his briefcase and opens it. He takes something out and puts it on his desk.

It's a brand-new nameplate that says FERNANDO.

The man sits there and gazes at his nameplate. But after a little while, he frowns.

The nameplate doesn't look quite the same as everyone else's. It looks different.

Cheaper, less official.

THAT day at lunch a problem develops. The man is sitting at his table, when another man from the office comes and stands over him. This man looks angry. Very angry.

Yes? says the man. What is it?

Why are you calling yourself Fernando? the angry man says.

The man thinks a moment. He clears his throat.

Fernando is my name, he finally says.

Fernando is *my* name! the angry man screams. He pounds his fist on the table.

More than one person can be named Fernando, the man says.

Fernando stares at him in fury. Then he leans forward over the table and hisses into the man's face.

You don't understand *anything*, do you? he says.

Then he overturns the man's lunch table and walks away.

The man falls to the floor under the weight of the table. He lies there for a while, in shock.

Everyone in the room is looking at him.

Maybe Fernando's not my name, the man thinks.

THAT night the man stands in his bathroom, cleaning the stains from his shirt.

How can I go on like this? he says. I need a name—I have to have a name.

Your name is Fernando, a voice says from behind him.

No, says the man. I tried that already.

Fernando, the voice says. Your name is Fernando. That's your name—*and it has always been!*

THE man goes to work the next day with renewed strength.

My name is Fernando! he screams.

The people in the office all turn and stare.

Fernando! the man yells. Do you understand?

The people nod their heads from behind their desks.

Nodding is not good enough! the man screams. If you understand what I'm saying—that my name is Fernando— then speak up! Say so! Right now!

We understand! the people say. Your name is Fernando!

Fernando! says the man. Fernando!

Fernando! the people say. Fernando! Fernando!

Just then Fernando enters. He is crying.

Please, Fernando says. You can't do this—it's wrong!

You are wrong, the man says. And stop crying!

I can't! wails Fernando. You're destroying me!

Who are you? the man says. You're nobody!

The unnamed man collapses to the floor, and the new Fernando strides about the room. He goes from desk to desk, snatching up nameplates and jamming them into his pockets.

I have all your names! he announces to the staff. I will hold them in my office. If you feel lost or confused, make an appointment with my secretary, and we'll fit you in as soon as possible. Now go back to work, and be quiet about it.

He goes into his office and slams the door.

FERNANDO, it reads, stenciled on the glass.

Fernando, forevermore.

The Ocean
Next Door

ONE NIGHT, THE woman has a dream that the ocean moves in next door. She can see it in there rolling around, as she stares out the window across the hedge. Somehow the ocean's all lit up from below—light's sparkling through the clear blue waves—and the white-capped peaks are moving back and forth.

And then the woman wakes up.

OH, the woman says quietly to herself, as she lies there in the dark.

After a while, she looks over at her husband. He's sleeping. Slowly, she sits up.

She gets out of bed and pads into the kitchen and pours herself a glass of water.

She peers out the window at the house next door. It sold months ago, but no one's moved in yet.

HONEY? says a voice.

The woman turns to see her husband standing in the doorway. He's wrapping his robe about himself.

Is everything okay? he says.

Oh yes, says the woman. It's just, I had a dream. I dreamt the ocean moved in next door.

The ocean, he says. I wonder what that means. Maybe you should go to the beach.

The woman smiles, and her husband smiles too.

I'll make you breakfast, she says.

He gives her a kiss and heads for the shower.

She makes coffee and toast and fries an egg.

But really, you know, her husband says—finishing his piece of toast—maybe you really should go to the beach. After all, that's what retirement's about.

I know, says the woman.

She sips her coffee.

Maybe I will, she says.

And after a while, she gives a nod.

It might be fun, she adds.

So after her husband has headed off to work, she goes and digs out her bathing suit. She packs it in a bag with a towel and a book, grabs her sunglasses, and gets in the car.

The beach isn't very far away at all, though the woman hasn't been there in years. She parks the car and walks down to the sand and finds a good spot to lie out. She puts on her sunscreen and sits there awhile, just staring out at the waves.

Well, she finally says, what are you waiting for?

She stands up and wades on out.

SHE swims a little bit, back and forth. The water's cool and the air is warm. Overhead, a few clouds and seagulls move by.

Then something brushes against her calf.

UGH, says the woman.

She moves her leg.

Probably just some seaweed, she thinks.

She peers into the water, but can't see a thing.

After a while, she turns and heads in.

SHE dries herself off and lies back down on the towel. She squirms a little bit. She feels a chill.

What am I doing here, anyway? she says.

She feels silly.

She decides to go home.

THE woman drives home with a headful of heavy thoughts. What is she going to do with her life? What's it all for? What's it all about?

When she gets home, there's a moving truck parked outside.

THE door of the house next door is open, and movers are carrying boxes in. The woman watches, then opens the door and walks up the path toward her home.

When she's almost to the door, she sees a man and a boy

on the neighboring path beside her. The boy's holding a bag and the man's carrying a lamp.

Hello there, the man says.

Hello, says the woman. Are you our new neighbors?

I guess we are, the man says. My name's Steve and this here is Johnny.

The woman goes over and shakes their hands.

Is it just the two of you? she says, looking around.

Yes, I'm afraid so, the man says.

I'm sorry, says the woman. I didn't mean anything.

I know, it's all right, the man says.

The woman invites the two of them for dinner.

I know moving days are hard, she says.

Thank you, says the man. We'd be delighted.

So would we, the woman says.

In her kitchen, the woman finds her apron and puts it on. She makes a salad and defrosts some steaks. When her husband gets home, she tells him the plan.

Sounds good to me, he says.

They all sit down around the table to eat. The man tells the two of them about his wife. They've decided to separate after fifteen years.

I have Johnny on weekends, he says.

~

WELL, says the woman, weekends are the best part.

Yes, I guess that's true, the man says.

Excuse me, he says—his phone's started to ring.

I'll take this outside, he says.

THE man goes outside and sits on the porch. They can hear the conversation through the screen. They can hear him quietly pleading with his wife.

Then the sound of crying floats in.

THE woman and her husband look at one another. The woman looks over at the man's son. He's staring at his plate.

She sets down her napkin.

Johnny, come with me, she says.

SHE leads the boy down the stairs into the basement. She opens the door to the storage room. It's filled with shelves of their children's old toys.

Do you see anything you like? she says.

THE boy's eyes widen as he looks around the room. Then he steps forward and starts to dig.

What's this? he says, after a while.

It's a miniature planetarium, the woman says.

See, she says, you put a bulb in here, and the light shines out through these holes. And it projects the stars all around the room. It's best at nighttime, of course.

ARE you sure? says the boy's father, when they go back upstairs.

The boy's holding the box in his hands.

Oh yes, says the woman. Please, of course.

These things should be used, she adds.

WHEN the good nights have been said and the neighbors have gone home, the woman and her husband do the dishes. Her husband washes and the woman dries.

They seem like nice people, he says.

Yes, says the woman. Yes, they do.

You know who else is nice? he says.

No, says the woman, but I have an idea.

I hope you're thinking about me, he laughs.

LATE that night, the woman has another dream about the house next door. This time it's dark—empty and run down— and there are old leaves blowing around inside.

BUT this time, when the woman wakes and pads out to the kitchen, and stands there pouring water into her glass, she looks out the window, and sees those lights in that room, like a tiny little universe looking out.

~

It's not a bad life, the woman says to herself.
    She reaches out and turns off the tap.
    Then she drinks her water and sets the glass down.
    And turns from the kitchen and swims out.

Zombies

THE MAN AND the woman are trapped in the house.

The zombies are trying to get in.

Aargh! Aargh! the zombies are saying.

The man and the woman don't know what to do.

Maybe there are some guns in here somewhere, the man says.

They search the entire house. But they don't find even a single gun. All they find is a knife, and it's dull.

Crap, says the man. I'm out of ideas.

The basement, says the woman. Let's hide!

THE man and the woman run down into the basement. They lock the door and huddle in the dark.

Upstairs they hear crashing and bumping and breaking as the zombies invade the house.

WHAT do we do now? the man whispers to the woman. Pretty soon they're going to come through that door.

I don't know, says the woman. We have to think!

Finally, the man has an idea.

I know, he says. Let's act like zombies!

You think it'll work? the woman says.

They practice staggering about with their arms out.

Aargh! Aargh! they keep saying.

MINUTES later, the zombies come through the door. They fall down the stairs and stand up.

The man and the woman continue their impersonations. They impersonate zombies for their lives.

THE zombies mill about in circles there with them.

Aargh! Aargh! everyone's saying.

The man and the woman seem to have escaped notice.

But then suddenly, the man starts to sing.

SHUT up! yells the woman. Have you gone insane? You're gonna get us both killed!

I'm sorry! says the man. It just sort of happened! This whole thing's so sad and depressing!

OF course, by now the zombies have noticed.

Aargh! they are saying. Aargh!

Run! says the woman.

They head toward the stairs, elbowing past zombies left and right.

~

LUCKILY the zombies are poorly coordinated, so the man and woman make it from the house. They run across the fields as fast as they can, with the zombies stumbling behind.

AFTER many miles of running, the man and woman take a break. They're both sweating and gasping for breath.

What the hell happened back there? the woman says.

I told you, says the man. I don't know!

WHEN they find civilization, they tell everyone about the zombies.

You should get lots of guns, the man says.

Yeah, says the woman, and stay out of the basement.

And keep your mouths shut, she adds.

THE man and the woman sit on a rooftop and watch the war against the zombies unfold. The zombies are slaughtered—they're a bunch of idiots.

The whole thing's pretty anticlimactic.

LATER that night, the two are lying in bed.

I can't believe we survived, the man says.

What were you singing? says the woman. I forgot.

Over the Rainbow! says the man, and they laugh and laugh.

Gorillas

I HAVE A FRIEND who paints pictures of gorillas—gorillas on bikes, chairs, horses, planes, kites.

Why are the gorillas always *on* something? I'd say.

He'd never answer; he'd just look away.

ONE day I found myself standing in his studio. He wasn't there; I don't know where he was. I was staring very closely at one of the paintings, when I suddenly noticed who the gorilla was.

DID you know he only paints *one* gorilla? I asked my wife when I got home that night.

Who? she said. Oh, yes, of course. Why, did you think there were different ones?

I guess I'd never really thought about it before. I always thought they were just paintings of gorillas. But now I couldn't stop thinking about them—picturing them. So many strange paintings of my painter friend.

FINALLY I decided to ask my friend about it.

Those gorillas look like *you*, I said.

Like me? he said.

He turned and looked them over.

Hmm, he said, I guess they do.

HE didn't really seem to want to talk about it.

A few days later when I went to see him, my friend was gone. I searched the whole house, from top to bottom. I went out back and looked around the garden.

Then I went over and asked his neighbors.

Haven't seen him for days, they said.

Last time I saw him, one of them said, he was right there, climbing up that tree.

I stood there and looked at the tree for a while. It was a tall tree, but not *that* tall. I would've been able to see him if he was up there.

But all there was was a single passing cloud.

A few months later, they auctioned his stuff off.

Owes a lot of back rent, his landlord said.

People took chairs and desks and lamps and books and tables.

I bought every painting he had.

~

THEY'RE on my wall now, hanging side by side. I'm standing here looking at them now. And the strange thing is—again—they look completely different.

Didn't these used to be gorillas? I ask my wife.

AND my wife looks at me, and then she turns away. She heads toward the stairs, with a little shrug.

I stand and watch her go. She looks different, somehow.

And her knuckles gently brush against the rug.

The Astronaut

THE ASTRONAUT HAS been marooned on the planet for he doesn't know how long. He lies in the shelter of the destroyed capsule, gazing out at the sand. He is running low on food and water; he can hardly move with his broken leg. The ship's beacon broadcasts a constant SOS, but the astronaut knows he'll never be saved.

One night the astronaut is awakened from his sleep by a dull pain in his arm. He looks over to see a strange batlike creature gnawing fiercely into him. He strikes out at the creature and it flies away—shrieking—into the night. But the pain in his arm grows worse and worse.

The skin is disintegrating by daybreak.

THE astronaut speaks to the ship's computer. It tells him he has been poisoned.

We can synthesize an antidote, the computer says, if a live sample creature can be found.

~

THE astronaut turns and stares into the distance. All around lie only desert and rock. Except for one spot in the very far west, where dark cliffs rise into the sky.

They must be up there, the astronaut thinks.

He finds the sample cage and sets out.

THE astronaut's broken leg is carefully bound, and he is a very strong man. But still, the going is extremely slow—and painful, even with medication. The bat's venom is coursing through his system. He knows it's just a matter of time.

When he finally reaches the cliff, he stands and stares up.

I'll never make it, he thinks.

He starts to climb.

THE astronaut climbs all afternoon. He pauses to breathe, to rest. Sometimes the sky seems to swirl around. The astronaut closes his eyes and prays.

WHEN he reaches the plateau, he sees a tree in the distance—an ancient tree, gnarled and tall. And hanging from the branches, like their cousins would on Earth, are dozens of the batlike creatures.

The astronaut slowly approaches the tree. The capture itself is simple. He zaps one of the bats with a burst from the stun, then shovels the fallen body into the cage.

The other bats rustle, but do not wake.

The astronaut turns and heads back toward the ship.

NIGHT falls while the astronaut is halfway down the cliff face. He strains to see by the stars. Inside his chest, the poison has found his heart. He feels it jump, stop, and start.

By dawn, the bat has awakened from its slumber and is gnawing at the bars of the cage. It screams as the astronaut approaches the capsule, whimpers as he carries it inside.

THE computer is ready. The astronaut prepares. He wrestles the bat from the cage. He pins it faceup, wings out on the dissecting tray.

Then he raises the scalpel.

The computer tells the astronaut where he must cut, the fluids and samples he must gather. The astronaut presses the blade to the creature's chest.

But just then he hears the sound.

It is a strange sound—piercing. High and clear. A whistle, almost a song.

The astronaut turns and moves to the door. He looks up into the sky above.

There, wheeling in the great empty blue, are hundreds—thousands—of bats. Revolving slowly in an unending stream. Calling down as if in a choir to him.

For a moment, the astronaut's vision seems to change as he stands staring up at the bats. For a moment, the circle they make in the sky is not them, but the Earth, his home.

~

THE astronaut turns and looks back inside. He stares at the creature on the tray.

He notices he still holds the scalpel in his hand.

After a moment, he tosses it aside.

SLOWLY, he drags the tray from the capsule. It is hard work; all his strength is gone.

He unpins the bat's wings and feels the wind as it flies.

And a space suit falls empty to the ground.

The Island

THE CAPTAIN HAS a map. He tells the men: There is an island—there are diamonds, rubies, emeralds. There is gold, there is silver. There are women, beautiful women—and so many birds, the trees are like rainbows.

The crew sets sail. They sail for many months. There are storms, gales, lightning, thunder. There are pirates, there is sickness. They run low on food and water. They lose their way. The stars are no help.

And at night, while the crewmen lie delirious in their bunks, the fog comes and whispers in their ears. The men try not to listen but the fog is insistent.

You're all going to die here, it says.

BUT then one day—miraculously—the ship comes to an island. The natives welcome them ashore, as if into a dream. There are castles made of diamond and towers cut from ruby rising high into the air. Food and drink, the likes of which the men have never seen, are brought to them on silver plates and in golden bowls. And there are women, beautiful women—women like angels—and so many birds, the trees are like rainbows.

The men are amazed. They fall to their knees.

Only the captain is unmoved.

This is not the island, he says. We sail tomorrow. There are no emeralds here, you fools!

THE crewmen are stunned. They stare at him in horror.

But the captain just turns and walks away.

In a panic, the men search the island all day long—but it's true, there isn't an emerald on the place.

AND that night, as they lie in bed, inside those diamond rooms, staring up at those ruby spires, the women of the island come and whisper in their ears: How could you ever leave this place?

BUT in the morning, when the captain stands waiting by the rowboat, as one, the men come out to meet him. They gather up the oars and they row out to the ship, and they climb up the rope ladder and in.

THE women of the island are wailing on the shore. The birds are shrieking, Stay, stay!

But the captain points his cutlass and the anchor is drawn up.

And the men turn green as glass as they sail away.

The Writer

ONCE THERE WAS a man who wanted to write, but he didn't know how to do it.

You just figure out the story and sit down and write it, everyone said. It's easy!

So the man sat down and tried and tried, but for some reason it didn't seem to work.

What's the story? he said. How do you know? How do you know what it is?

THEN one day the man saw on the news that a famous writer was in town. He was giving a reading at the local bookstore.

I'll go ask him! said the man.

AT the reading that night, the man sat and listened politely while the famous writer read. And afterward, he raised his hand.

I would like to be a writer, he said. But for some reason, I just can't do it. I'm having trouble with the story part. I don't understand how you know what it is. How do you know what to write?

The famous writer sat there and looked at him.

Well, he said, it's easy. You start at the beginning, and let it unfold. When you get to the end, you walk away.

OKAY, said the man, and went home to his desk. He sat there and stared at the page.

But what's the *beginning*? he said in frustration. None of this makes any sense!

THAT night the man drove to the next town over, where the famous writer was doing another reading.

But how do you know what the beginning is? he yelled, when the writer had finally closed his book.

The writer sat there and looked at him.

Look, he said. You listen. You sit very still, and listen to your heart. When your heart speaks, you start taking dictation.

So the man went home and grabbed some paper. He sharpened his pencil and sat down at his desk. He closed his eyes and took a breath, and listened to the inside of himself.

He stayed like that for a long, long time, but nothing at all ever happened. He waited and waited for his heart to speak.

This is stupid, he finally said. I'm going walking.

~

So the man stood up and walked out the door. He walked down the path to the road. And then he turned and just kept walking. He never once looked back.

He walked and walked across the town, and then across the state. And then he just wandered aimlessly.

Sometimes he traveled freight.

He lived that way for many, many years. He went everywhere, met people, did things. He was always busy; he had no time to stop and think. It never even dawned on him to sleep.

But then one night the man was in a bar, and he saw the famous writer in the back. The writer was laughing and drinking with friends.

The man stayed there and watched them all night.

And when the writer left, the man followed him discreetly—from a distance, like a detective on TV. And when the writer turned in to his fancy hotel, the man watched for a light to go on from the street.

Late that night, the man broke into the writer's room, and stood over his bed in the dark. He looked at the writer lying there before him.

Then he knelt and pressed an ear to his heart.

~

HE listened and listened to the writer's heart all night, and then, in the morning, he rose.

You lie, he whispered.

And the writer smiled.

And that, he said, is *exactly* how it goes.

The Woman, the Letter, the Mirror, and the Door

ONE DAY THE woman gets a letter in the mail. She opens it up and starts to read.

I am your long-lost twin, the letter says. Please, would you like to meet me?

The woman takes a breath. She stares at the letter. She has always wanted to meet her long-lost twin. But still, she finds her hands are shaking.

She gets up and goes into the bathroom.

Should I go? says the woman, to the woman in the mirror. Should I go? Should I meet my long-lost twin?

The woman in the mirror considers for a moment.

Then she simply shakes her head.

THE woman tears the letter up and throws it in the trash. She tries to go on with her life. She sits in her house and acts like nothing's happened.

But a week later, another letter arrives.

~

PLEASE, the letter says. I've waited my whole life. I'd really like to meet you while there's still time.

The woman turns her head in the direction of the bathroom.

Then she grabs her keys and quickly sneaks outside.

THE woman drives across town to the address on the letter. She parks outside and stares at the house. She opens her compact to check on her makeup—and finds the woman in the mirror staring back.

WHAT are you doing? says the woman in the mirror.

I'm going to meet my long-lost twin, the woman says.

No you're not, the woman in the mirror says loudly. You're going straight home, right now.

No I'm not! says the woman. I'm tired of doing what you say. And I'm tired of always being alone.

You always were selfish, says the woman in the mirror.

In answer, the woman clicks the compact shut.

SHE opens the car door and stands looking at the house. She walks up the walk and rings the bell.

After a while, footsteps can be heard.

The door opens, and a man is standing there.

~

THE man and the woman look at each other. They look almost exactly alike. After a while, the man starts to smile.

Would you like to come in? he says.

THE woman goes inside. She stands there in wonder. The inside of the house looks exactly like her own. The woman can't believe it. She looks at the man.

What's the matter? he says. Is something wrong?

No, says the woman.

She looks toward the bathroom.

Do you have one too? she says.

One what? says the man.

The woman looks at him.

Oh, she says. Never mind.

THE two sit on the couch. The man talks for a while, but the woman finds she can't concentrate.

Will you excuse me a minute? she says, putting down her cup.

Oh yes, of course, the man says.

THE woman stands up and goes into the bathroom. For a moment, she stands staring at the floor.

Then she steels herself and looks up, into the mirror.

But the woman in the mirror isn't there.

~

THERE'S nothing there, in fact, on the other side of the mirror—it's just the bathroom, empty, with no one in it. The woman looks down at herself to be sure.

Then she stretches one hand toward the mirror.

THE mirror gives a ripple as her hand moves right through it—continues right through to the other side. The woman pulls her hand back, stares at it a moment.

Then she climbs up onto the sink.

ONE leg first, and then the other, and then the rest of her, the woman moves through the mirror's frame.

She emerges into the other bathroom.

Then she turns, and looks in the mirror again.

AND now, there in the mirror, the woman sees herself—just her reflection looking back.

Hello? she says—and her other lips move too.

Then she hears a knock.

EVERYTHING okay? says a voice.

The woman, startled, turns. She realizes her brother's outside the door.

Oh yes, she says. I'll be out in a minute.

Actually, come in here! she calls out.

~

THE knobs turns, and the door opens, and her brother's face appears.

Come here, come here, the woman says.

He walks into the room. They stand before the mirror.

Just look at this, she says.

FOR a moment, the two of them stand looking at each other.

Then he smiles, and she smiles too.

Can I tell you, he says, how I finally found you?

And she says yes.

And her reflection says it, too.

Wings

THE MAN MEETS a woman and falls in love.
I want to marry you, he says.
And he does.

SOME time goes by, and everything is great, but then one day the man is walking by the bathroom, when he looks inside and sees his wife with a pair of white wings on her back.

Wings? the man says, looking at her in confusion. I didn't know you had wings.

It's best not to talk about it, his wife says with a smile.

She quietly closes the door.

BUT what are they for? the man says at dinner. Where do they come from—and where do they go?

They're not really wings, his wife says after a while. Please don't ask me anymore.

~

THE man becomes irritated. Frustrated. Angry. Why is she keeping things from him? All this time, he's loved her so much, and now this—it's so strange.

Mystifying.

TIME goes by. The man starts working late. He has an affair with his secretary—it's just physical. He comes home at dawn and slips into bed.

But he never sees his wife's wings again.

AND finally one morning the man wakes up and finds that his wife is gone. He searches the whole house, looking for a sign, a note to explain—anything. But there's nothing there—and nothing is different. Her clothes are in her closet; there's her car. It's just her, she, his wife who is missing.

He can't understand where she's gone.

THEN the man tilts his head and looks toward the window. He steps outside and stands on the lawn. His gaze drifts up to take in the sky.

And that's when he has his idea.

IT takes some time—a month or two, three—but the apparatus now is all set. The man straps it on and straightens his goggles.

He revs it and lifts off the ground.

~

AT first his flight is extremely peaceful, just a few birds moving here and there. But as he rises, other forms appear, whirling about like leaves in the air. There's Mrs. Kilcannon, who disappeared three weeks back; there's Rodney, the Tastee Freez manager. There's Julia Barth, he hasn't seen her in years; and Lucius—Hey Lucius!—from Florida.

The man vrooms about, back and forth, searching through the thickening sky, while the other fliers glide on past, their eyes locked on their own personal plight. For a while, it's a nightmare, just churning confusion, but then it all stops, and suddenly widens—

And there's the man's wife, falling from the sky—

And there the man goes, sharply diving.

HE dives and he dives—the machine's to the limit—there's the ground coming up, there's his wife. And he catches her then, at the very last minute, and touches down, clinging to his life.

The Lemon Tree

A FARMER WAS WALKING through his orchard at harvest time, when he saw an apple hanging from one of his lemon trees. He frowned at it awhile, and then went and fetched a ladder, and climbed up and plucked it from the branch.

LOOK what I found in one of the lemon trees, he said to his wife when he got home that night.

Very funny, she said.

No really, said the farmer. This apple was growing from one of the lemon trees.

I'm not stupid, said his wife. Don't be ridiculous.

The farmer looked at her, then down at the apple. He raised it to his mouth and took a bite.

It tastes like lemon, he said.

He looked at his wife.

Don't you want to try it? he said.

You must be out of your mind, she said.

And then she stood up and walked out of the room and went back to doing the laundry.

In the morning, the farmer went back to the tree, and examined it with a great deal of care. There were no more apples growing anywhere on it, but he could still see the spot where his had been.

Guess I'll just have to wait, the farmer said.

And wait was exactly what he did.

A whole year went by, and the farmer was very busy—he worked so hard, he forgot the whole thing. But the next harvest time, as he was walking through the lemon trees, he saw another apple.

In fact, two of them.

This time the farmer went and got his wife.

I want you to see this, he said.

He dragged her through the orchard and showed her the tree.

That's the same tree as last year, he said.

The farmer's wife stood there and stared at the apples.

Well what does that prove? she said. Anyone could've glued those apples up there. They didn't grow there, for sure.

And she turned and left.

So before the start of the next harvest time, the farmer got everything set up. He arranged a pair of cameras—one on either side of the tree—and aimed them at where the apples had been.

Have you completely lost your mind? his wife said.

Just want some documentation, the farmer said.

But of course, when the fruits all ripened on the tree, there were only lemons—no apples in sight.

THE farmer couldn't believe it. He went out there every morning, and stood looking, watching, waiting, all day long. He went over the pictures with a magnifying glass.

And his wife packed her bags and drove off.

So long, she said. I'll send you the divorce papers.

But the farmer hardly seemed to hear.

He went back inside and sat down on the bed.

I should think about something else, he finally said.

AND so, after that, the farmer thought about other things. He read some books, traveled around, learned to paint. He played a little golf, became proficient at the banjo, built a shortwave radio at age seventy-eight.

AND when the farmer finally died, he was all alone, and hadn't left any instructions as to what should be done. And so the people buried him beneath the apple tree that stood alone amidst the lemons of his farm.

Elmore Leonard

ELMORE LEONARD WAS a famous writer, but this isn't a story about him. This is a story about my friend Elmore Leonard, who wasn't a famous writer at all. Oh, he was a writer, my friend Elmore Leonard; he just wasn't a famous one. I don't know if he was a good one either, because he never wrote anything.

He tried a lot; he tried really hard. He had a fancy typewriter and everything. It was one of those ones that comes in its own suitcase, in case you ever go anyplace.

Not that Elmore ever left his mom's house. He was too busy waiting for inspiration. He'd just sit there and sit there, staring at the page.

I don't know what I'm doing wrong, he'd say.

I remember one day, I finally got up the nerve to say that maybe Elmore wasn't *meant* to be a writer. I mean, maybe his talents lay in other directions?

But Elmore didn't want to hear about that.

I just can't help but feel, Elmore said in a loud voice, that with a name like *Elmore Leonard*, I'm destined to be a famous writer.

And it was hard to argue with that.

ELMORE had a job at one of the factories, and he stayed clean and sober, so it didn't really seem like that big a deal that he wanted to be Elmore Leonard the famous writer. After work he'd come home and sit at the typewriter for a while, and then I'd come over and we'd drink beer. It was harmless, like how some guys play in bands on weekends, or some people always read the newspaper.

BUT then, one day, everything changed. One day I went over to Elmore's house, and he came up to me carrying a book.

Look what I wrote, he said.

I looked at the book. It was an Elmore Leonard book. *Rum Punch*, I think. Maybe *Maximum Bob*.

This is an Elmore Leonard book, I said.

Exactly, Elmore Leonard said.

AFTER that, Elmore had to go live in the hospital. His mother was very upset.

What's wrong with him? she kept asking me.

He thinks he's Elmore Leonard, I'd say.

SOMETIMES I'd go see him, and we'd sit in the visiting room. They wouldn't let him have any of "his" books. I remember one time he was reading Edgar Allan Poe.

This guy's crazy, he said.

He asked me if I could sneak him in one of his books, and I promised him that I would try. And I did, but unfortunately I was caught, and then they put me on the Do Not Visit list.

After that, Elmore and I sorta drifted apart. Neither of us were too big on writing letters. I think Elmore might've sent me a postcard one time, but I'm not sure, because there was nothing written on it.

FOR a while, nothing happened; time just passed. I went to work, came home, watched TV. But then one day I saw that Elmore Leonard book sitting there—the one I'd tried to sneak in to him at the hospital.

The book was on the couch, where I'd thrown it that night. I don't know why, but I picked it up and started to read. I'd never really read a book before then. I mean, unless it was for school or something.

And the thing of it was, the book was really good! It was funny; it made me laugh. It was about these two guys who tried to rob a bank and then one of them got caught and put in jail. But the thing about it I liked was that the characters were good; it really seemed like they were best friends. They had fun, even when they were running from the cops. Except of course for when the one guy was in prison.

So I read the whole book, and then when I was done, I just sat there, staring at the cover. Staring at that name there—my friend's name on the book. That name that had caused him so much trouble.

And as I was looking at it, a thought came to me. It was a thought that I'd never had before. So I got in the car and drove to Elmore's mom's house.

Why'd you name him Elmore Leonard? I said.

AND Elmore's mom looked at me, and then finally she frowned.

It was his father's idea, she said.

She opened the door and ushered me in.

She motioned toward the wall with one hand.

I'D been in Elmore's living room a million times before, but somehow I guess I'd never seen it. I knew the walls were lined with shelves of old books.

But I'd never noticed they were all Elmore Leonard novels.

His dad sure did love those, Mrs. Leonard said. He used to sit there and read them, and laugh and laugh. That is, of course, until the day he finally left. That was when Elmore was three or four, I guess.

I stood there and stared at those books on the wall. Then something happened: I started to cry. And Mrs. Leonard heard me and turned in surprise.

Well, what's wrong with you? she said.

THE way she said it, it's hard to describe. It almost sounded like she was mad. Mad at *me*—like I'd done something wrong.

It's nothing; I'm sorry, I said.

~

I excused myself and went on home. I drank a beer and tried to watch TV. But after a while, I turned it off.

I went to bed, but I couldn't sleep.

I just lay there in the dark, thinking about Elmore, and about those books on the wall. About Elmore's father sitting there reading them and laughing. And then the silence that must have fell when he was gone.

And then I started thinking about the characters in that book. How they were friends and stood by each other every day.

And then I thought of Elmore sitting up there in the hospital.

And I knew I had to get him out of that place.

So that night I went out and put gas in my car. Made sure everything was running fine. I went to the bank and took all my money out.

Then I drove to the hospital and put the ski mask on.

I went in through the roof; it wasn't really that hard—took a crowbar to a rusted old lock. There was a guard but I hit him with the butt of my dad's hunting rifle.

Come on Elmore, I whispered. It's time.

WE ran down the stairs and burst out the front doors; we were halfway to the car when the sirens started to whine. We peeled out of the parking lot, past the first cop cars as they came, took the shortcut through the hills to Route 9.

~

WE were screaming down the highway at 110; I remember the needle going all the way off the dial. There were helicopters and searchlights; I don't know how we got away. There was just this voice in my head saying, *Drive, drive.*

THE sun was rising as we crossed the state line, and I became of aware of this kind of noise. I looked over and saw that Elmore's mouth was moving.

Pull over, he was saying. We're all right!

WE stopped by the side of the road and just sat there for a while. My knuckles were still white on the wheel.

Thank you, Elmore said. I can't believe you did that. No one ever came back for me before.

OH hell, I said, you would've done the same.

But Elmore just shook his head.

Maybe, he said, but I kinda doubt it. Let's find a gas station, though—I gotta go.

A few miles down the road we pulled into a mini-mart; I grabbed a case of beer and a couple of Snickers bars. On the way up to the register I noticed Elmore looking strange. He was standing there, staring at the newspapers.

I walked up beside him. He'd gone completely white.

What is it? What's the matter? I said.

Then I looked over his shoulder and saw that huge headline.

Elmore Leonard the famous writer had died.

OH, I said.

Then I looked at Elmore.

But it's okay, though, I said. It isn't you.

I know, Elmore said. I'm better now, you know. It's just, he meant a lot to me, is all.

I picked up the newspaper and paid for all the stuff, then we went outside and sat in the car. We drank a few beers and ate the Snickers bars, while Elmore read the obituary aloud.

It was all about the life of the real Elmore Leonard— how he was born in New Orleans and grew up in Detroit. How he went to a Jesuit school and then joined the navy. How he had almost fifty books in print. But the best part came when they talked to his friends, and they told all these stories about his life. From the way they talked, you could tell they really liked him; you could tell Elmore Leonard was all right.

And at the end of the article, it talked about his funeral, which was gonna be the next morning at eleven o'clock.

We could make it, Elmore said. I mean, we'd have to drive fast, but it's not that far, just Detroit.

~

BUT Detroit? I said. That's back the way we came. We'd be crazy to go back through there.

And I looked at Elmore and he looked at me.

And we laughed, and I put the car in gear.

Acknowledgments

"THE DODO" WAS written on a commission from the Selected Shorts Commissioning Project.

The first line of "The Madman" was lifted (with love) from Michael Moorcock's *Behold the Man*.

"The Ocean Next Door" was written under the spell of Dennis Etchison's "Keeper of the Light," which can be found in his collection *Red Dreams*.

Dennis Etchison also appears (in disguise) as the famous writer in "The Writer."

Many thanks to my agent, Sarah Funke Butler, and to Allison Lorentzen, Diego Nuñez, Patrick Nolan, and Paul Buckley at Penguin.

The following people helped tremendously with these stories: Andra Moldav, Barbara and Mel Loory, Cecil Castellucci and everyone at Nine Pines, Fiona Dourif, Garrett Ehring, Mary Hamilton, Maureen de Sousa, Paige Stewart, Rachel Andersson, Steph Cha, and Tommy Moore.

Thanks also to the following for various major assistances: Adam Ross, Aimee Bender, Alex Maslansky and Claudia Colodro at Stories Books and Cafe in Echo Park, Allison Scoles, Asadollah Amraee, Bud Smith, Cameron Pierce, Carla Richmond Coffing, Catherine Feeny, Cedering Fox and everyone at WordTheatre, Charles Yu, Chris Bachelder and everyone at the University of Cincinnati (especially Mica, Michael, Justine, Luke, and Liz), Chris DeWan and the California State Summer School for the Arts, Colton Haynes, Conrad Romo, Darice Cadriel, David Evans, David Gill, Eduardo Santiago, Ellen Datlow, Gabe Durham, Gina Srmabekian, Hanne Steen, Heather Chapman, Heather Donahue, Hugh Schulze, Ikoi Hiroe, Ira Glass and everyone at *This American Life*, Jacob and Rina Weismann at Tachyon Publications, Janelle Ricci, Janet Fitch, Jean-Paul Pecqueur, Jeff McClure, Jeff VanderMeer, Jeffrey Ford, Jen Michalski and Phuong Huynh, Jennie Hettrick, Jessica Lauren Richmond, Jessica Sugar Kiper, Jillian Lauren, Jim Ruland, Joe Hill, John Skipp, Joseph and Sondra Blair, Julia Garcia Combs and the Deacon, Juliet Escoria, Justin Hamacher, Kate Bernheimer, Katherine Ayars, Katherine Minton and Jennifer Brennan at *Selected Shorts*, Katy Flaherty, Kayden Kross, Kelly Link and Gavin Grant, Kevin Incroyable, Kit and Joe Reed, Lauren Candia, Lea Thau, Libby Flores, Liev Schreiber, Linda Venis and everyone at the UCLA Extension Writers' Program, Liza Trombi, Liz Gorinsky, Mackenzie Hoffman and everyone at Clockshop, Marcia Gay Harden, Maria Dahvana Headley, Maria Rodriguez, Marilyn Friedman and

Jeff Bernstein at Writing Pad LA, Mark Haskell Smith, Mars and Melissa Sandoval, Martin Pousson and everyone at CSUN, Matthew Berger and everyone at Cal State Fullerton, Matt Rowan, Matty Byloos and Carrie Seitzinger, Megan Kurashige, Meg Howrey, Melody Chang, Michele Franke and everyone at PEN Center USA, Mickey Pando, Nathan and Andy Hudson and all the wonderful musicians at Stony Brook, Nick Bonamy, Pegah Savehshemshaki, Peter Straub, Phoebe Lim, Ransom Riggs, Rick Wilber, Robert Swartwood, Ron Carlson, Ron Currie Jr., Rose Fox and everyone at Readercon, Roxi Gasaway, Sabra Embury, Samantha Dunn, Scott McClanahan, Sean Carswell and everyone at CSU Channel Islands, Sean Pessin, Simon Cottee, Stacy Valis, Steve Rasnic Tem, Sydney and Andy Duncan, Todd Petty and everyone at the College of New Jersey, Tod Goldberg and everyone at UCR Palm Desert, Vi Ha, Xach Fromson, Zoe Ruiz, everyone who wrote blurbs, everyone I thanked last time around, and everyone I forgot.

Plus a very special thanks to Matt Chait—

"Who cares what someone else did?"